THE THROWBACK: A WESTERN DUO

THE THROWBACK:
A WESTERN DUO

Cherry Wilson

GUNSMOKE

First published in the US by Five Star

This hardback edition 2011
by AudioGO Ltd
by arrangement with
Golden West Literary Agency

ISBN 978 1 445 85674 2

British Library Cataloguing in Publication Data available.

Printed and bound in Great Britain by
MPG Books Group Limited

Table of Contents

Foreword   7

Montana Rides   11

The Throwback   108

Foreword

Although Cherry Wilson is virtually unknown today, over the course of her writing career she produced over two hundred short stories and short novels, numerous serials, and five hardcover books. Six motion pictures were based on her fiction. Readers of *Western Story Magazine*, the highest paying of the Street & Smith publications where Wilson was a regular contributor, praised her stories in letters to the editors and ranked them next to those of Max Brand.

Wilson was born Cherry Rose Burdick on July 12, 1893 in rural Pennsylvania. When she was sixteen, the Burdick family moved to the Pacific Northwest, and Cherry remained a Westerner for the rest of her life. She married Robert Wilson, and for a time the two led a nomadic existence. After Robert fell ill in 1924, they took up a homestead near Republic, Washington.

Prior to Robert's illness, Wilson had written for newspapers and tried her hand at Western fiction. One of her first stories, "Valley of Sinister Blossoms," appeared in Street & Smith's *Western Story Magazine* (8/27/21). Now, to support them, Cherry became a full-time writer. Although Street & Smith would remain her principal publisher over the course of her writing career, around this time she also began contributing stories to Fiction House's *Action Stories*. Her story, "Guns of Painted Buttes", appeared in *Action Stories* (10/25) and was named Third Prize Winner in the Authors' Popularity Contest sponsored by the magazine the year it appeared.

Among her early stories were a series of interconnected

tales about the cowhands of the Triangle Z Ranch that emphasized humor and male bonding. She varied the series by borrowing an idea from Peter B. Kyne's THE THREE GODFATHERS (1913), making her cowpunchers co-operative caretakers of an orphan in seven of the stories. Wilson stressed human relationships in preference to gun play, although action was often supplied by rodeos, horse races, or wild horse chases. Some of her best work can be found in those stories where the focus is on relationships between children and adults, as in her novel, STORMY (1929), and short stories like "Ghost Town Trail" (1930) — a fascinating tale with an eerie setting and a storyline filled with mystery which can be found in THE MORROW ANTHOLOGY OF GREAT WESTERN SHORT STORIES (Morrow, 1997), edited by Jon Tuska and Vicki Piekarski — and "The Swing Man's Trail" (1930) in which a boy doggedly pursues a herd of rustled cattle that has swept up his family's only cow.

In 1936, not long after she was widowed, Wilson gave up the homestead and moved to Hollywood, California, where she lived until early in 1938 when she moved to Spokane, Washington. She was still living in Spokane when she died on November 18, 1976 at the age of eighty-three.

The two short novels that make up this duo — "Montana Rides" from *Western Story Magazine* (12/17/27) and "The Throwback" a three-part serial from *Western Story Magazine* (4/20/29–5/4/29) — were both made into movies in the 'Thirties. It is not surprising since both stories include rodeo action and center around young male protagonists, each trying to prove something to himself and win the hand of the girl he loves. For the film version of "Montana Rides" the title was changed to THE SADDLE BUSTER (RKO, 1932). Tom Keene was cast in the role of

Montana, a hill-raised boy who wants to become a champion rodeo rider. The screen version is a very faithful rendering of Wilson's storyline and characters, with names intact, and it still remains a charming, if at times sentimental, movie.

The adaptation of Cherry Wilson's serial "The Throwback" was altered in several ways for the film version, THE THROWBACK (Universal, 1935), although its title was retained. Buck Jones was a popular movie cowboy in the 1920s and 1930s who made four of the six films based on Cherry Wilson stories — THE BRANDED SOMBRERO (Fox, 1928) [based on Cherry Wilson's short novel, "The Branded Sombrero," in *Western Story Magazine* (5/14/27)], EMPTY SADDLES (Universal, 1936) [based on EMPTY SADDLES (Chelsea House, 1929)], SANDFLOW (Universal, 1937) [based on "Starr of the Southwest," a three-part serial in *Western Story Magazine* (7/25/36–8/8/36)], and THE THROWBACK. Jones was also responsible for bringing Wilson's novel STORMY to the attention of Henry MacRae, a producer at Universal, which was filmed under this title in 1936, starring Noah Beery, Jr., and Jean Rogers. Because Jones had an established movie cowboy persona, elements of the story were altered to make it a Buck Jones vehicle. The hero's name was changed from Jess Trailor to Buck Saunders; upon the killing of his father, he is sent away and raised by a rancher, and together they establish one of the biggest ranches in the West; and the story's broncho riding episode was altered to a horse race.

This is the first time that "Montana Rides" and "The Throwback" have appeared in book form since their publication in the pulps over seventy years ago. They both demonstrate what it was that readers loved about the writing of

Cherry Wilson: her humor, her humanity, her love and respect for animals and for the West.

Vicki Piekarski
Portland, Oregon

Montana Rides

I
"OUT OF THE HILLS"

Just as the April day reached its zenith, two riders descended the cool, timbered heights of Crazy Mountains and came out onto the spring-flushed prairies of Painted Buttes range. Hill folks, they were, as their homely dress proclaimed. Yet seldom were two riders encountered who made a more distinct appeal to the heart and eye. Nor yet two more unlike, although with a curious spiritual likeness that made it fitting, somehow, that they should journey like this together, and the one incongruity that they should ever part.

One was an old man, hoary of hair and beard, on whose gaunt face time had written its seamed story — written deeply, indelibly, for there were no lines of shame to hide. His eyes, beneath their white brows, were like fine flame, reflecting now some light of dread or sorrow. His head and feet were bare. But despite this, despite the fact that he rode, bareback, a very small and nondescript mule, he achieved a rude dignity that was most impressive.

His companion, in sharp contrast, was a youth of twenty years or so, Indian straight and dark. His delicately chiseled features were still, as an Indian's are still, but it was the stillness that the solitudes school rather than the mark of a tranquil heart. For the boy's heart was a volcano, and the fires of it flamed in his dark eyes, impelling his lithe body to strain forward in the saddle as to some wondrous goal, even as he held in the mustang to the mule's slow gait.

"I can do it, Jude!" Eagerness made tremulous his tone. "I can do it . . . if only I get my chance!"

But the old man shook his snowy head in gentle reproof. "Boast not thyself of the morrow, son, for no man knows what the day may bring forth." He looked like some old patriarch from out of the ancient book he quoted.

The boy's spirits would not be damped. "It ain't boastin'," he argued earnestly, "to say you can do what you know you can. An' I'll do it, too . . . not tomorrow, but today . . . if only he'll take me, Jude!" His very intensity made that last a prayer. "We'd be rich, Jude!" Again his heart overflowed to fill the empty void. "You wouldn't have to herd goats for a livin'. I'd look out for you, Jude! You wouldn't have to do a thing but sit up there alone, readin' your book."

"Alone!" The sorrow of Abraham, of all fathers who have given their sons as a burned offering on the altar of life since time began, was in the old man's voice.

The boy said with answering pain: "I'd miss you, too. You've been mammy an' pappy both to me since . . . I'd be a snake," he cried passionately, "if I ever forgot you, Jude! But if he takes me, I'll come home often. There won't be any good byes between us, Jude."

The old man did not reply. He knew their good byes had been said — that the only real separation was that of spirit.

"I wouldn't even try for the chance without your say-so, Jude. But ever since I went down to the Coulée City roundup last spring, an' seen fellows doin' the sort of thing I've been doin' for years . . . doin' it for fun . . . an' them gittin' money an' name for it, too, Jude. But you was against it till jist of late, an' I. . . ."

"I wanted to keep you on Angel's Peak," old Jude said wearily. "I was selfish, son, and in my selfishness I sinned. For it was a sin to hide your talent from the world. It came to you from the Almighty, and must not be buried, but returned unto Him manyfold."

Slow miles the mule and mustang plodded.

"What if he won't even try me?" worried the boy. "What if he won't believe I can ride . . . ride *any* horse? But he will if you tell him, Jude. He'll believe *you*. He ain't like to remember me . . . for I wasn't but a kid when he used to visit us at Angel's Peak. But I recollect him right plain, an' his girl . . . the li'le redhead, with the boy's name, Sonny. Once I told Sonny Hurn her hair looked like ripe strawberries in the sun, an' she slapped me, Jude. I ain't forgot how her father laughed. But it was," he added thoughtfully, "that kind of hair."

So, smiling now at that old memory, they rode. At every turn in the trail, Jude's old eyes sought the blue-misted hills to which he might soon return — alone. But not once did the boy look back. It was as if, for him, the hills had served their purpose. Nothing told him that, in the high tide of his young pride, he was to creep back to them, seek out their darkest depths and hide, as the wild things hide when their death wound is on them. His eyes were set from them in gladness and hope.

Then hope and gladness merged into a great anxiety that grew at every step. Far across the plains he saw the buildings of the Big Horn Ranch, and over them a tornado of dust that rolled and fumed — the dust of conflict, dust that was the very breath of life to him. Only out of such a wild welter of blood and sweat and dust would come the great end he sought.

For Big Horn Ranch — in summer, just another of the peaceful cattle ranches that dot the Montana plains — was the winter home of Hurn's Wild West Show, and its training ground in spring. Now, in mid-April, a place of frenzied action, of continuous excitement, where devil-may-care young humans lived only, it would seem, for one joyous, wanton flirtation with death. And to be one of them was the hill boy's dream.

Breathed there a boy the wide West over, who did not dream that dream? To be a Horn rider! Numbered among such famous cowboys as Calgary, Kid Clagett, and the new member, last year's Northwest champion, Ranse Gaines. In company with cowgirls as renowned, particularly Rita Sills, sweetheart of the rodeo, and the rodeo king's own winsome daughter, Sonny Hurn. To be associated with horses whose names were household words, and equally popular with rodeo fans — War-Path, See-Saw, Yellow Peril — Yellow Peril, whose infamy eclipsed the others' fame. That great, man-killing demon, whose very name was potent to send a chill up the spine of the gamest rider in the West.

A dazzling company! Probably the only person who could be dissatisfied with it was the man who was responsible for it, Dan Hurn. For while his men, as a group, ranked highest in the rodeo world, individually they fell short of his great ambition.

For Dan Hurn, too, dreamed a dream. His dream was nothing less than to produce a rider who would crash his way through the host of top-notch riders, and come in first at Pendleton and Cheyenne — to produce a world's champion. But, although he had trained many men — good men — for one reason or another the dream of his life had failed, year after year, until it had become a maxim with rodeo folk that a contract with Dan Hurn hoodooed a rider's chances for the championship.

For years he had sought a rider to break that hoodoo. This year, *this hour,* a young rider neared Big Horn Ranch. Was he the man for whom Dan Hurn watched and prayed? If so, would Hurn recognize him, in homely guise, coming, as he did, out of his own hills, unheralded and unsung?

II
"A FRIEND AND A FOE"

Hurn's Wild West Show wasn't a "show" in the strictest sense of the word.

"You furnish the frills," Dan Hurn advertised, "and I'll supply the thrills!"

And supply them he did, in the form of bucking horses so lawless, and riders so daring and skilled, that towns from Kamloops to Chihuahua, desirous of their local stampede, fair, or other celebration, bid briskly for Hurn's rodeo, keeping the outfit, from June until late autumn, continuously on the road.

Today Hurn was trying out a shipment of wild horses in the hope of finding a few of sufficient savagery to merit a place in his famous outlaw string. Horse after horse, fresh from the range and indescribably vindictive in its first hate of man, was ridden to its own defeat, or to the Waterloo for the cowboy who had fought for the honor of riding him first.

"*Yip-ee-ee-e!*" roared a dozen dusty, lusty throats, as a wild pinto, with Calgary aboard, plunged from the chute into the corral, staging a cyclonic exhibition of bucking that made even that hardened audience gasp, and the cowboy, to save himself from a disastrous spill, ingloriously snatch for the saddle horn.

Mighty good horse, thought Dan Hurn, *to make a rider like Calgary pull leather.* More than satisfied with its showing, he blew his whistle, the signal for the pick-up man to race alongside and lift the cowboy from his pitching mount.

Sheepishly Calgary was ambling back to the fence, running the gamut of good-natured gibes at having pulled leather on a green horse, when a big, blond, flashy-looking buckaroo loudly jeered: "Oh, mama, git him a hobby!" Both his look and tone conveyed an insult. "An' he calls himself a *rider!*"

Pausing, Calgary shot Ranse Gaines a glance of cold contempt. "Aw, chase yourself! You blamed well know this ain't ridin'! Hurn's tryin' out hosses, not men. I could 'a' rode him to a standstill! But if I'd 'a' set him one buck after that whistle blew, I'd 'a' got my time!"

Ranse's lip curled in a supercilious sneer: "Great ol' alibi . . . Hurn's whistle!"

Calgary's muscles tensed dangerously, and for a moment it looked as though he would resent that insult with his fists. But he only shrugged and walked on to join his pals.

"Dan," solemnly predicted old Keno, the ranch foreman, to Hurn, who had missed this byplay, "your star rider is shore gallopin' to a fall, and, when he falls, he'll fall hard."

Dan Hurn's shrewd eyes narrowed swiftly. "How come?"

"He ain't been with this outfit but three weeks," said Keno bluntly, "but to see him strut you'd think he owned it."

"Hot young blood just naturally loves to strut," reminded Hurn, with something strangely like relief.

"All right, let him strut," conceded the foreman gracelessly. "But our boys ain't the kind that'll stand bein' rode over roughshod. One of these days there'll be trouble, an' Ranse will be in it."

"I can't have that!" Hurn's voice took on an edge. "We've got to pull together an' pull with a will to break that hoodoo. Ranse is our one chance. The boys know that."

"They do," admitted Keno. "They're as keen for it as you are. They've et dirt right along to keep peace in the family. But they's a limit to the dirt an *hombre*'s supposed to eat . . . a peck a lifetime, accordin' to statistics. Goin' on the ration, the boys has over-et every day since Ranse showed up."

"A little dirt won't hurt 'em." Hurn smiled. "I've been bankin' strong on Ranse ever since he won the Northwest Championship last year. An', while he ain't exactly a man after my own heart, he sure can ride."

But Keno was stubborn. "It takes more'n good ridin' to make a champion," he pointed out, still eying the hope of Hurn's outfit with frank dislike.

"Yeah," agreed Hurn earnestly. "It takes skill, strength, cold nerve, an' a likable nature that gets the crowd. But it's easier to find a needle in a haystack than a man who combines all them points. Which I ought to know, if any man does . . . havin' hunted just such a rider the ten years past. Lord, if I could find him. But I guess it ain't in the cards. The years go by, an' I don't get any younger. What with this hoodoo scarin' the ambitious youngsters off, I consider myself lucky to have Ranse. He's got everything it takes, but the personality."

"Sure of his nerve?" Keno put in idly, and Hurn took him up in a flash.

"Mean to say you ain't?"

Disconcerted by the direct query, by the tense way Hurn awaited his reply, Keno shifted uncomfortably. "I dunno," was his honest admission. "He takes his hosses as they come, but . . . Dan, he's a bully, an' I ain't seen a bully yet that wasn't a coward at heart. I hope I'm wrong. But, if you're groomin' Ranse for the championship, let me give you a tip . . . see that he cuts out sentiment an' gits down to cases. He's lettin' Rita make a fool of him."

Hurn's sternness relaxed at that, and a genial grin overspread his face. "Pretty hard to stop a heart-free *hombre* from gittin' sentimental over Reet," he reckoned, looking at the vivid, dusky-eyed beauty in red, queening it over Ranse and the group from her throne on the fence.

Nevertheless, when work was resumed, Hurn watched his star rider closely. This talk with Keno had him worried. It wasn't Ranse's unpopularity that bothered him, for he could trust the boys to keep friction at a minimum out of loyalty to the outfit. Nor was he disturbed over his obvious infatuation for Rita Sills. What did upset him was the foreman's hunch that Ranse lacked nerve. He meant to back Ranse in his race for the championship, but — if there was one tinge of yellow in his make-up, it would crop out to his certain defeat in the finals. And another disappointment. . . .

"Run in that black," he ordered the ranch hands, forcing his mind to the task at hand. "If he's as bad as they say he is, his heart's as black as his hide."

Perhaps this introduction led the rodeo crew to expect too much. For the black's appearance in the chute — so meek and cowed, in comparison with his warring predecessors — was greeted by whoops of glee. And in inverse ratio to his docility was the cowboys' desire to ride him.

"I'd be ashamed to take advantage of him," was the way Calgary put it. Then, as his eyes met Rita's and lighted with mischief, he innocently suggested to Hurn: "He's a nice,

18

tame, li'le ladies' hoss . . . give him to Reet."

The girl flashed him a scornful look that was full of coquetry, nevertheless.

"Oh, is that so?" she drawled, sliding down from the fence. "Since when have the ladies of this outfit asked any favors when it comes to horses? Forgot all about Sexton over in Spokane, have you, Cal? He piled you so high you had to use a parachute to get back, but . . . this lady rode him!"

"I'll say she did!" loyally backed Sonny Hurn.

"Yeah," grinned Calgary, as a laugh went up at his expense, "she did . . . by a rattlin' good exhibition of *he*-ridin'!"

Enjoying that as much as any, Rita was bending to pick up her saddle when Ranse Gaines stayed her, and himself lifted it to Keno, a-straddle of the chute fence. Not even then, as Dan Hurn frowningly observed, did he relinquish it quite, but, after it was on the sleepy-looking black, tested the cinch by a tug or two, as if he could trust the girl's safety to no one else.

But surely, Hurn thought, he could be forgiven for that, galling as it was to the other boys. For the girl, sitting there in the saddle and sun, in her shimmering scarlet blouse, her dusky hair confined with a band of the same bright hue, and the same rich bloom in her cheeks, was enough to make a monkey out of any man.

"Careful, Reet," he cautioned, observing a slight twitching in the black's shoulder muscle. "You can't always tell about the quiet ones."

"You bet you can't," took up Calgary, with the freemasonry that prevailed in Hurn's happy family and was enjoyed by their employer as much as any. "Recollect that sody jerker down in Tucson, who was so quiet he had to yell seven times to make a whisper, till he fell so strong for Reet, he. . . ."

"While that banjo-totin' Mex down Salinas way," put in Kid Clagett impishly, "what hung around Reet pickin' catgut an' yowlin' how *hees* heart was a-blaze, a-blaze, till Ma Hurn doused the conflagra. . . ."

"Cut that!" In the jealous rage he felt at mention of any and everything that had touched the girl's life before he met her, Ranse Gaines whirled on Kid. "If you yahoos don't know how to treat a lady, here's one *hombre* what aims to teach you!"

Dan Hurn saw Kid's face go cold, and he was about to interpose when Kid got the better of his anger, and he himself got a new conception of how much the boys would do to further his dream by the game way Kid tried to turn that affront into a joke.

"Whoopsla! You been insulted, Reet," he informed the girl, with his slow grin. "Say, Ranse, if you knew how many scalps that li'le gal's lifted besides your own, you'd. . . ."

"Shut your mouth and open your eyes," cried Rita, as Keno, at a hasty signal from Hurn, swung the chute gate, "and watch a *lady* ride!"

"When?" Calgary called maliciously, as moments passed with no slightest movement on the part of the black.

But before the words had fairly left his lips, a streak of black and crimson shot out of the chute, tied itself into a knot in mid-air, and snapped out of the knot with a terrific force that sent the girl, completely off guard, crashing over his head to earth.

There was one second of horror while she lay stunned, and the black, a dynamo of venomous action now, reared over her, and it was an even chance whether the pick-up's rope would snare him before those crushing hoofs descended. But the rope won, and Rita was up, coming back to the fence slapping the dust from her britches, so chagrined that not even Calgary had the heart to tease.

The horses in the adjoining corral, maddened by all this excitement, were milling in a body so compact that it defied the best efforts of ranch hands to cut out any particular one, when. . . .

A great, raw-boned buckskin emerged from the jam and walked deliberately toward the chute.

Instantly Keno sprang to the opening and was wildly waving his hat to frighten him back, when he caught an all but imperceptible signal from Hurn to let him come. As he scrambled to safety, the mighty outlaw stepped into the pen.

Strange, the change that came upon Hurn's riders then. No banter now, no mad rivalry to be the first to ride him. Nothing after the first astonished gasp, but silence, and an infinitude of that. All eyes turned expectantly on Ranse Gaines. He was the top rider, as he never let them forget. All right. Let Ranse ride him, it wasn't their funeral.

Dan Hurn, too, looked at Ranse, and in his eyes was an agony of suspense. But he could make nothing of the cowboy's face or bearing. There was nothing to show that Ranse realized, what everyone else had guessed — that he was put to the test. Indifferent to their combined gaze, he leaned indolently forward on the fence, watching.

Yellow Peril! The outlaw who no man ever rode. Of the many who had tried, two had died. And another — the most promising rider Dan Hurn ever trained — had been so badly crippled that he would never set foot in the stirrup again. Yet here stood the great, tawny brute, watching them with red, villainous eyes. Wise with awful wisdom. Arrogant with awful reason. Unspeakably more deadly for these encounters, a living challenge to a duel with death.

Would Ranse Gaines take that challenge? Breathless, they waited the answer, while age-long seconds passed. Back of each for Hurn lay ten years of bitter failure. On each hinged his great hope of redeeming success this season. He didn't intend — wouldn't allow — Ranse to ride him. But Ranse must *want* to. Must prove his nerve. What was going on in the cowboy's mind? Lord, if he only knew! Surely this minute he'd. . . .

"Prince of the powers of evil" — out of the blue came that voice, addressed to the outlaw stallion, so soft that it struck the heart rather than the ear — "thy name should be legion for there are many devils in thee."

As they dumbly stared, the speaker turned from Yellow Peril to them — a gaunt old man on mule-back, whose flowing mane was silver in the sun and whose eyes beneath their white brows were like fine flame. Eyes to pierce the soul, to read thoughts masked from the eyes of other men.

"Jude!" boomed Dan Hurn, striding toward him and taking his hand in a hearty grip. "Waal, you ol' hermit, tell me what good wind brings you here?"

The old man said gently, as the rest drew up: "You used to talk some, Dan, of wantin' a star to set in your crown . . . a rider, above other riders. Is it still a wish?"

"It's a craze!" cried Dan Hurn fervently. "Next to bein' a star, Jude, is the honor an' glory of creatin' one. Time an' again, I've set up my star, only to have it eclipsed by a brighter. But this year . . ." — his eyes sought Ranse, amusedly watching this tableau from the fence, and his voice fell away.

"This year," completed Jude, his eyes seeking the boy who had come up with him and was, as yet, unseen, "you will win."

Fierce joy shot through Dan Hurn as if it were a prophecy come true. "You predict that, Jude." Strange that he should put so much faith in the simple old recluse of the hills. "You think I'll. . . ."

Then he saw the boy, sitting his mustang a little apart. There was something wild and wistful in his face that took Dan Hurn back to a mountain shack and a mountain lad.

"Montana!" he cried, going up to take the boy's hand. "Waal, bless my soul, if you ain't man-grown! An' you weren't nothin' but a willow shoot last time I saw you."

Some recollection of that visit crinkled the fun wrinkles about his eyes and, sweeping back a long arm, he drew his daughter, Sonny, up to confront the visitor.

"See here, Monty," he chuckled, running a rough palm over the girl's rich, bronze hair — for this was a favorite joke with Hurn — "it don't look much like a strawberry now."

It was a most unfortunate reunion for the two. For this public airing of their childish quarrel put a constraint upon them that it would take much to dispel. Seeing their embarrassment, aware that he had blundered somehow, and seeking to cover it, Dan Hurn caught Rita Sills by the shoulder and swept her up.

"Here's a young lady," he said jovially, "who eats up that stuff, Monty. You can tell Rita her head looks like a ripe strawberry, and I'll guarantee *she* won't slap you."

The hill boy looked at Rita's lustrous, jet-black hair, and convulsed them by his earnestness and answer: "But it ain't!" he protested. "It's midnight . . . in the starshine!"

He flushed deeply at their mirth, and deeper yet, although for a pleasanter cause, when the girl laid her hand over his upon the bridle. "Something tells me, Monty" — and Rita's dusky eyes and cheery lips smiled up at him —

"that you and I are going to be great friends."

Ranse Gaines, left with Yellow Peril at the chute, both heard and saw. The cold, impersonal hate of the outlaw horse for man was scarcely less dangerous than the jealous hate the star rider instinctively felt for the boy, Montana.

III
"A FAVOR HE WON'T FORGET"

Aside from his jealousy of Rita, it was only natural that Ranse Gaines should hate the hill boy at first sight. For Montana was everything that he was not, hence, to one of his warped and envious disposition, instinctively antagonistic. Who was he, Ranse wondered — that young buck, who looked like an Indian and dressed like a scarecrow? He burned to know. But it wasn't about Montana he made indifferent inquiry when Keno came back to the chute.

"Who's the ol' gazaboo on the jackass?" he asked, and was genuinely amazed at the way the old foreman bristled up.

"Gazaboo?" Keno echoed slowly, as one repeats a sacrilege. "Ranse, I'll pass that up, because you're a newcomer here an' don't know. That's Bible Jude . . . the good Samaritan of Painted Buttes."

"The which?" Ranse permitted himself to be mildly curious.

"The good Samaritan . . . the *hombre* what helps poor folks which nobody else wants to bother with, not for money, but just outta love for his fellow man."

"Oh, Bible stuff!" scoffed Ranse.

"An' danged good stuff anywhere you git it!" Keno said hotly. "Now, lookee here, Ranse," — taking that cowboy by

24

the shirtfront with a none too gentle hand — "Jude may talk queer, for he lives more in the Gospel than in this day an' age. He may *be* queer. But he's all wool an' a yard wide. Folks respect him because he practices what he preaches. An' they'd about make hash outta the *hombre* what hurts his feelin's. What's more . . . he's done so many good turns for so many folks hereabouts that you won't make any moves without steppin' on some of them. So it behooves you to step right easy around Jude. Savvy?"

"When he's done a good turn for *me*," sneered Ranse, jerking away, "mebbe I will."

"Mebbe he's done you one already," Keno said, with a meaning glance at Yellow Peril — "comin' up when he did."

Brick-red at that thrust, Ranse's eyes involuntarily sought Dan Hurn. The rodeo man and Jude had drawn a little apart and were in earnest converse, and the cowboy wondered guiltily if he were the subject of that talk.

But it was of Montana they spoke — or rather Jude spoke, telling Dan Hurn something of the boy's deep longing and preparation for a rodeo career.

"You know what his life has been," Jude quavered, with a reluctance that was in itself convincing — "a wild life and a lonely one. He's had to make his own fun, and he's made it all these years in trappin' an' ridin' the wild mustangs of the hills. He is a born rider, and by steady practice . . . Dan, I never saw his like. I never told him that. I hoped he'd never know. But he saw your rodeo at Coulée City last spring . . . saw the world was hungry for talent like his. And he's been crazy ever since to ride for you. Take him, train him, and may he be the star you seek."

Of that, Dan Hurn had little hope. Good riders were common as thistles on the plains. The one he sought correspondingly rare. However, if the boy was a good rider, he could use him. Yet he hesitated, fiddling with his watch fob, his eyes afar. Rodeo life was a dangerous life in more ways than one. And Jude, despite the long intervals between their meetings, was Dan Hurn's friend.

"It's a hard life, Jude," he said seriously. "A ruinous life for some."

The old man's face, as brown and sere as a withered leaf, darkened with the shade of sorrow. "It's his choice, Dan . . . not mine," he said sadly. "I've done my best to hold him, but he's heard the call of life. Till it's answered, there's no happiness for him at home."

"Then," said Hurn, his conscience clean, "he'll have his chance."

With Jude, he walked back to the expectant group, he was touched by the way the boy's black eyes fairly leaped to meet him.

"I'm givin' you a try-out, son," he said kindly, laying a hand on Montana's shoulder. "If you make good, I'll take you on. But you'll find rodeo hosses a heap harder to handle than wild mustangs. All a wild hoss knows about fightin' is what's born in him. Mine have been educated in the art. So don't take it to heart, if you don't make the showin' you'd like."

It was all Montana could do to jerk out the one word: "Thanks!" For joy choked him, suffocated him, as he removed his saddle from the mustang with trembling hands. *He was to have his chance!*

Understanding just how big this moment was in his life, Hurn left him, and, going up to Keno, ordered Blackjack brought in for the test. Then he turned back for a word with Jude.

With unusual decorum, his riders draped themselves

over the corral fence. It was always interesting to see a new rider do his stuff, and they sensed that this was no ordinary rider, would be no ordinary ride. They liked Montana and wanted to see him make good. Also, they were generous enough to tell him so as he came up with his saddle in his arms, and his dark face shone with pleasure. But there was one who did not wish him luck.

As Keno stooped to withdraw the bars and drive the man-killer back into the pen, and so make room for the horse Hurn had designated, Ranse Gaines interfered.

"Why not the buckskin?" he suggested. "Make it a real test . . . give the kid a *hoss!*"

"You heard him!" cut in the blond rider, with an unpleasant smile. "An *hombre* has a right to pick his hoss! Put his saddle on Peril!"

That name caught Dan Hurn's ear, and he whirled on Ranse.

"You fool!" he stormed, angrier than any of them had ever seen him. "You'd put a new man on a hoss you wasn't in any hurry to tackle yourself! What are you tryin' to do? I said Blackjack!"

Unable to put up any defense, Ranse stared back with reddening face at Hurn. It was a painful moment for all. Then the hill boy interrupted.

"I'm sorry, sir," he told Hurn quietly, "but I said I'd like to take a whirl at him. I might not ride him, but I'd make a hard try."

"You're up for trial, lad . . . not execution," Hurn said shortly.

But he liked the boy for trying to shoulder the blame, for his willingness to ride a horse that even a novice could see was deadly. Montana had nerve. He knew how to play the game. Two mighty good qualities, and the ride not started.

Hurn was conscious of some impatience as he waited for Blackjack to be driven in.

He had picked this horse — a big-boned black — because he was a strong, jarring bucker who could keep up the racket longer than most. What he wanted to observe was the boy's riding style and ability to stand punishment. To him there was something heroic in Montana's coming out of the hills to fight for a place among the best riders in the West, with nothing but courage and confidence to back him up. Something pitiful in his battered saddle, now going on, so frequently repaired that little of the original leather was left. He would have offered him a better weapon for this fight but feared to hurt his pride.

He saw red again, as Ranse Gaines — smarting under his humiliation, seeing his chance to humiliate someone else, and mean enough to take it — swung up on the fence as Montana eased into the saddle, snatched off the boy's hat, and held it up to the general gaze. It was an old slouch hat and, like the boy's whole get-up, cheap in the first place, and pathetically, ludicrously dilapidated in this.

"Holy tripe, kid!" he cried in affected astonishment, gingerly holding the hat between forefinger and thumb. "You sure don't aim to ride Blackjack in *that!*"

It was a cruel spectacle, yet no one moved to stop it. Hazing a new rider was permissible, even ritual, although seldom did it carry such a sting. The respect awarded Montana in the future would depend on the way he handled Ranse now. Calgary and Kid were sick with disappointment as the boy — so they thought — swallowed the bait. But Dan Hurn was not so sure.

"Us rodeo riders," went on the bully with huge relish, "are mighty choosey about our hats. Ever notice that?"

Meekly Montana admitted he had, but never knew why.

"Because," volunteered Ranse, "a rodeo hoss won't buck unless he's fanned with a real hat. The better the hat, the harder they buck. Blackjack would lay down an' quit, if you tickled his ears with a last year's bird nest like that! See mine?" Removing his own hat, a costly, gray sombrero, he held it up beside Montana's as if to shame him by the contrast. "I won the Northwest Championship with that hat last year."

"It's right purty," admired the boy with a humility that made Calgary groan. "It's sure some hat."

Ranse offered, rubbing it in: "I'll loan it to you for this ride. Don't say I never done you a favor, kid."

With the proper show of deference, Montana accepted the sombrero. Then the blindfold was jerked off Blackjack's eyes. The gate swung. And, in that split second while the horse poised, the watchers were astonished to see the boy's arm fly out and the sombrero sail into the dust of the corral. Almost in the same instant the outlaw leaped out, a screaming, writhing meteor, and, as Ranse Gaines sprang to the fence with an oath, Montana called, from the crest of a high, twisting buck: "I'll get it . . . as I go by!"

Sure that this was bravado, the crowd watched, breathless. They saw the boy's spur flash to the outlaw's shoulder and back. Saw the horse involuntarily swerving from the steel — land, with a shock that shook the corral, right beside the hat. In that brief flash, before the angry brute plunged into another reeling toss, they saw the boy's lithe body sway in a downward arc, and him retrieve the hat, regain his balance, and wave it about the ears of his furiously bucking mount. Then bedlam broke loose at the fence.

Not one of them could do that trick on a *bucking* horse, one time in fifty — certainly not on Blackjack. Yet this boy had done it the first time, and with amazing sang-froid and grace. Then the hat episode fled their minds in stark wonder at his riding.

His riding! They had no words for it then or thereafter — for the sheer, cold nerve Montana displayed in this first ride. That was what impressed them most. For it took nerve to stay with Blackjack, as they knew so well. To go up with his mighty, wrenching heaves, to stand the jar when he came down with the stunning force of the weapon for which he was named. To endure those tearing, torturing bucks that had all the great brute's size and strength behind them. Even a moment of it was killing. Yet moment after moment the boy stayed on.

"Ride 'em, cowboy!" they screamed wildly.

"You show 'em, Monty!"

Dan Hurn was climbing the corral, yelling to the awful *thud, thud, thud* of Blackjack's hoofs: "I'll back him against the best of 'em! Against the world!"

Still the boy stayed with it. Through the enveloping dust, they caught the sun glint of his spurs — brief flashes of his face, dead-white and set — the swing of his arms as he fanned the borrowed sombrero about the frenzied outlaw's ears.

But, as the battle waged, they ceased to cheer, and gripped the fence, straining toward him, as if in that way to help him to endure.

Two had watched in silence from the start — Ranse Gaines, now with twofold cause for jealousy — and old Jude of Angel's Peak, in sorrow, at the lonely future to which Hurn's enthusiasm had set the seal. As separate in the way they viewed the struggle were Rita Sills and Sonny Hurn. Rita's eyes were luminous, and constantly she fought nearer. But Sonny ceased to watch, was at last unable to bear it, and tugged at her father with the cry:

"Stop it, Dad! Stop it!"

But Dan Hurn didn't hear. He was oblivious to all things, save that he had found the rider he had prayed for all these years — a rider with skill, strength, grace, personality, and nerve. A rider after his own heart. A champion!

"Against the world!" he raved above the uproar, feeding the black hate in Ranse's heart.

But, seeing some sign of weakening in the horse, remembering that a rodeo horse ridden to a finish was ruined for his purpose, he blew the whistle, and the pick-up man lifted Montana from Blackjack's back.

Pale, shaken, with wavering, uncertain steps, Montana came back to them and straight up to Ranse Gaines. "Thanks," he said, handing back the sombrero, "that's a favor I won't forget."

Leaving Ranse to decide for himself if the words held gratitude or threat, he passed on, to be overwhelmed by Hurn's outfit, and given a rousing welcome into the fold.

"You're great, Montana! Great!" cried Rita, her lovely face very close to his. "You'll fade us all out of the picture!"

Again Ranse saw and heard. Who could tell what awful thoughts ran through his heated brain?

Eyes that read things hidden from other men busied themselves with reading. Old Jude's muttered comment on what he read sent an icy chill of foreboding through Dan Hurn: "A stone is heavy and the sand is weighty, but the wrath of a fool is heavier than both."

IV
" 'WAKE UP, RANSE!' "

Having seen Montana enrolled as a member of Hurn's Wild West Show, old Jude went back to the hills. The boy accompanied him part way. For the most part, it was a silent ride. Montana, dazed by his good fortune, dazzled by glowing pictures of the new life ahead, felt both pity and remorse at the thought of Jude's returning to the lonely shack and to what seemed to him now, by contrast, the drab and dreary life of the wild. In this silence they came to the first steep rise, the parting place of mountain and plain, and Jude pulled up his mule.

"You'd better be gettin' back, son," he quavered. "You ain't your own man no more."

Still they lingered, loath to part. It was nearing sunset, and the big, golden disk was resting on Angel's Peak, but down here they stood in the mountain's shadow. Suddenly it struck Montana that Jude was looking unusually old and frail.

"Son, remember that Dan Hurn is your master. Serve him with heart and hand and head. And remember. . . ."

"Yes, Jude?" as the old man faltered.

Jude stared fixedly at the boy before him — so fine, clean, young, so eager on life's threshold — and his face settled into deeper seams of worry. Did Jude foresee the future? Did he know that the warning he was about to utter was too late?

" 'The lips of a strange woman,' " he said, with moving solemnity, and strangely fell those words on the boundless Montana plain, " 'drop as a honeycomb, and her mouth is smoother than oil.' "

With a simple handshake, he was gone. A great warmth

stealing over him, Montana watched the old man slowly climb from shadow to sun until the sun-goldened mists on the mountain crest caught him up in a cloud of glory. Then, smiling to himself, the boy headed back for Big Horn Ranch.

The lips of a strange woman — *Rita's* lips. Jude had heard Rita praise him. It *was* sweet — sweeter than the honey of the wild bees. But Jude hadn't meant it that way. He meant something serious — like he always did when he used Bible talk. Jude meant he should be on guard around Rita. Folks sure did get queer about women. The phrase kept singing through his brain — "The lips of a strange woman. . . ." — and his eyes kept seeing the red, laughing lips of Rita Sills.

Montana was in love. There was no mystery in that. For he was simple, elemental, unversed in the ways of women, while the rodeo girl was an adept in the game of love. She had made an effort to attract him, and her smile had been as a spark in the tinder — a fire, easily lighted that might not be so easily put out.

When two miles from Big Horn Ranch, he caught a flash of crimson through the green boughs, and came upon her *waiting there where two trails merged; his heart leaped for joy and surprise. Rita's surprise seemed even to exceed his own.

"I usually take a gallop at sunset," she fibbed, as her horse fell into step with his mustang on the trail. "Isn't it lovely, Montana?"

All but speechless at the sheer loveliness of it, the boy said: "Yeah!"

He wanted to tell her how lovely it was to be riding with her. How lovely *she* was. How he'd never seen a sunset half so lovely before. A thousand really vital things like that.

33

But. . . . "It's sure lovely," he stammered, "to belong with you-all!" Nor dreamed he had expressed them all.

"Oh, it's a great life, if you don't weaken," she laughed. "Always on the move . . . a new town every few days, new crowds, new friends, new thrills. You poor kid." She leaned toward him to give his hand a consoling little pat. "It must have been awful . . . living up there in the sticks with that old dodo."

But Montana didn't like that, the pat notwithstanding.

"I ain't sure what a dodo is," he said loyally, "but, if you mean Jude, he ain't one."

"A dodo's a bird that's been dead a long, long time," Rita said gaily. "So he is one . . . a nice, funny ol' dodo!"

Montana found himself laughing with her, and it gave him a guilty twinge.

"It wasn't awful . . . not till I got the rodeo craze," he said honestly. "I had lots of fun . . . catchin' wild hosses, ridin' 'em, huntin' an'. . . ."

"Don't tell me!" protested Rita, with a pretty grimace of distaste. "I know just how thrilling that was, for I was raised in the hills myself. I go home every now and then for a visit, but about one week of it is all I can stand."

"How long have you been with Hurn?"

"Three years. And take it from little sister, this is the life! There's no limit to how far you can go, if you've got the goods. Take Ranse Gaines. The salary he makes Hurn pay him is a hold-up. But Ranse deserves it . . . for he passed up a chance to act in the movies to ride for Hurn."

The boy's heart was torn by a cruel and unfamiliar pain. "Think purty much of Ranse, don't you?" he blurted.

"He likes *me*," countered the girl roguishly. "But he don't like you, Monty. He tried to put you on Yellow Peril . . . that awful man-killer . . . when he knew. . . ."

34

"I'd 'a' rode him, too," boasted the boy, half wild at her harping on Ranse. "I didn't know what he was . . . then. But I'd 'a' rode him! An' I will ride him some day . . . soon."

Thrill crazy, heedless of the mad flame she was fanning, Rita encouraged: "I'll bet you could. I'll have a reserved seat in the grandstand when you do. But, say, Ranse will sure hate you then."

"I'll make out," promised Montana. His heart was in his eyes as he added softly: "I don't care who hates me . . . you said we'd be friends."

Wiser in the ways of love, Rita answered lightly: "Oh, you won't care about me when we hit the road. You'll find plenty of girls willing to be friends with a good-looking fellow like you. Don't blush, Monty . . . you will. Then you'll forget all about poor little me."

"When I forget you," cried the boy tensely, "I'll be dead!"

Rita didn't laugh at that. His honesty disconcerted her, but this very simplicity was his charm. Content to let their first real talk rest on the high point, she said little more, nor did he, on the rest of that ride home.

From the ranch house piazza, Dan Hurn saw them coming.

"By George," he chuckled to Sonny, who sat on a lower step, her head resting against his knee, "Rita ain't lost no time. She's roped Monty, or I miss my guess."

Sonny sat up to watch the couple.

They had dismounted, and Rita gave her reins to Montana so he could put up her horse. Starting up the walk to the house — for the girls of the outfit lived there, under the motherly protection of Ma Hurn — she caught sight of Ranse Gaines scowling from the bunkhouse door, and out of pure deviltry ran back to Montana and whispered something in his ear. He nodded eagerly and led the horses off. Rita ran up the path, greeted the two on the piazza, and passed on into the house, merrily singing that famous classic:

> And when the moon shines over the cow shed,
> I'll be waiting at the k-k-kitchen door!

"Wonder what she said to Monty," smilingly speculated Hurn, "to make his face light up like a meetin' house on Sunday night?"

"Nothing very weighty," ventured Sonny, who had been wondering, too. "Rita's boy crazy. She'd make eyes at good old Jude just to keep in practice."

"Kitty, kitty!" teased her father, surprised at her disparaging her chum.

"That was catty," Sonny owned candidly. "She doesn't mean anything by it, Dad, but the boys think she does, and they break their hearts discovering she hasn't any. Just the same, I wish she'd left Montana alone."

"Love's like the measles, honey," philosophized Hurn, amazed that she should make an exception of the new rider, "everybody gits it. An' the younger they git it, the easier it is on 'em, as a rule. Monty'll be plumb cured before we break trainin'."

Sonny's sweet face was serious. "Some don't get over it, Dad."

"No," he admitted thoughtfully, "some don't. Now an' then a case is fatal. Who you afraid for, chickabiddy?"

He hadn't realized how earnest she was till she lifted her face to him now in the dusk.

"Ranse," she said slowly. "Dad, he's wild about Rita. He

36

looks daggers if a man as much as speaks to her. And he hates Montana already. Remember how he tried to get him on Yellow Peril? And, Dad, there was the queerest look in his eyes when Montana gave him back that hat. I'm afraid Ranse's case may prove fatal . . . to someone else, for if Montana and Rita. . . ." She broke off with a little shudder. "I'm afraid, Dad."

But nothing could worry Dan Hurn long. He felt sure in his soul that Jude was right — that Montana would be the star in his crown when his rodeo days were done. That the boy would break the hoodoo, would fulfill his lifelong dream, by being the Hurn rider who would lead the world. Besides, he knew now and frankly admitted to himself, he had never been any too sure of Ranse.

"Thank heaven," he exclaimed irrelevantly, "that *my* girl ain't got a tumbleweed rollin' around in her head instead of a brain!"

"I don't know that sense is anything to be thankful for," said Sonny, with a bitter tinge that troubled her dad.

After she went inside, he walked up and down in the gathering dusk, thinking it out in his slow way. What was wrong? Sonny wasn't a bit like herself tonight. He'd never seen her show a trace of spite before. She couldn't be jealous of Rita, for there wasn't any call for her to be. She hadn't Rita's dash, but she was far prettier in a sane, sweet way. There wasn't a man in the outfit who wouldn't have died for Sonny Hurn. Probably she didn't want Montana to suffer, either from Rita or Ranse.

When Sonny was just a little thing, he'd taken her along on his trips to see Jude. She and Montana had been great playfellows then. They'd had their spats, like all kids, but they'd kiss and make up. He remembered now how she'd talked of Monty for years. No, Sonny wasn't one to forget a friend. And now when the boy had shown up, man-grown, and couldn't see her for Rita — naturally that *would* hurt.

As he reached this point in his cogitations and walk, he saw Rita slip out on the porch with something white in her hands and duck around the house. A moment later he saw Montana leave the bunkhouse and circle around toward the kitchen, too. There was something just a little guilty in their movements, and Dan Hurn, deciding to see what was up, bent his steps that way. There was light enough for him to see what they were doing through the wild cucumber vines that framed the stoop, and, after one look, he beat a hasty retreat, shaking with inward laughter.

So that's what she whispered to him, he thought, chuckling to himself. *Nothing weighty, is right. No wonder his face lit up, or he met her at the kitchen door. Reet sure knows the way to a man's heart. Huckleberry pie! They're stuffin' it down three rows at a time. Swiped it, too, by thunder. Say, won't ma raise Cain. Go to it, kids, you're only young once.*

He was still enjoying their prank, when he made a turn in the walk again, and a man, night-blind or blinded by passion, ran into him headlong. Hurn caught him by the arms and held him off.

"Wake up, man," he said jovially. Then his blood ran cold. For if ever he saw murder on a man's face, he saw it then on the face before him. He said, each word biting as a whiplash: "Wake up, Ranse!"

V
" 'I'LL RIDE HIM!' "

Now there opened up for Montana a new heaven and a new earth. After his solitary, uneventful life, it was wonderful to have companions of his own age and tastes. Their jargon, the pranks they played on each other, the way they lovingly reviled each other, were to him a continuous delight. He tried to overcome his shyness, to get the kinks of the solitudes out of his tongue, that he might join in, but found it difficult. However, he did fall easily into the hectic routine of Big Horn Ranch. Daily he rode one or more of the outlaws, and, as he developed, Hurn was more and more convinced that he had the makings of a champion.

When, at times, Montana tried to realize what it would be like when he was riding before packed grandstands that had paid to see him ride, his imagination fell short. He could think of nothing more glorious than this. Something doing every moment and each moment better than the last, although a few of them loomed over the rest as Angel's Peak loomed over Painted Buttes range.

There was, for instance, the soul-satisfying moment when he put on the habiliments of his new life — the blue shirt, the yellow bandanna, the fifteen-inch sombrero with its nifty center crease — *the chaps.* Leather chaps, with wide wings!

He passed up breakfast that morning, so he could have privacy to study himself in the bunkhouse mirror while the boys were at the cook shack. But the chaps didn't show in the glass. However, by bending forward, a hand on each knee, he could see them pretty well for himself.

"Gee," he whispered rapturously to his glorified legs. "Gee!"

It wasn't true. He was still dreaming — about being a rodeo rider for Hurn. If he pinched himself, he'd wake up. But he didn't want to wake up — to the cabin in the hills and nobody but Jude, where one day was just like another, only each a little more dead than the last. He wished Jude could see him in chaps. His shining eyes went to the heap of garments on his bunk — the old clothes he had worn when he came — and his heart swelled with gratitude as he thought of how Dan Hurn had come to him last night with these new clothes over his arm.

"Thought you might not want to wait till pay day to git into rodeo togs," the boss had said offhandedly, "so I rounded these up. I know just how much kick a young fellow gits out of lookin' the part."

But Montana knew Hurn wanted to spare him another humiliation like the one he'd got from Ranse. And he had a mighty yearning to show Hurn how much he appreciated it — prove that he was fit to wear these clothes. He wanted to do something big for Hurn — like riding Yellow Peril. He could ride a Kansas cyclone — in chaps! And Rita — he'd look a heap different to her in this outfit. More like a regular rider — more like Ranse. Again that cruel pain tore through him.

Absolutely without vanity, merely in an effort to see himself as Rita would, he turned to the glass again. Clothes sure did make a difference. Of course, he admitted to his smiling reflection, his shirt wasn't silk like Ranse's, and his hat wasn't as flossy, still. . . .

"Right han'some," allowed a dispassionate voice in his rear.

Blushing furiously at being caught in such an act, Montana pivoted to see Kid, Calgary, and the rest lined up behind him, looking him over from sombrero to toe, as critically, solemnly as stock judges inspecting a prize steer.

"Yep, he's plumb han'some," decreed Kid again, and they all confirmed it by an unsmiling nod.

"Still an' all," pointed out Calgary, judicially fingering his chin, "han'some is, as han'some does."

They gave this due consideration. "Waal, he done right han'some on Blackjack," Kid decided, "so we'll let him live."

"Aw, shucks." Montana grinned foolishly. "Go on. I like it . . . from you."

He felt more like one of them when they joshed him like that. He'd noticed they never did Ranse. Missing his rival, he asked idly when they went outside: "Where's Ranse?"

"On Reet's trail," opined Calgary, throwing a fraternal arm over Montana's shoulder, "or sulkin' by hisself. Thank the Lord, he don't herd with us."

But, as they went up to the corrals to turn the peaceful ranch into a bedlam for the day, they saw him. Again he was leaning against the fence, staring at Yellow Peril. Staring hard, unseeingly, like a man in a spell — an evil spell, for he was deaf even to their boisterous approach. When Kid slipped up behind him, slapped him on the back, and sang out with the innocent sweetness that is always a mask for cowboy deviltry — "Still thinkin' it over, Ranse?" — the big fellow recoiled with a start that startled the boys, and a countenance so dark and ugly, so distorted by guilt, that he might have been convicted of manslaughter on his looks.

"Oh, Ranse is one of them slow, deep thinkers," razzed Calgary, no longer bottling his dislike, now that Hurn had a rider who outshone Ranse. "About the time we hole up next fall, he'll make up his mind to ride, or not to ride."

"Ride him yourself," shot back the cowboy, "if your mind works faster."

Calgary responded imperturbably: "I don't lay no claim to bein' a champ."

Ranse's bold, blue eyes insolently swept Montana from head to foot. "How about the hillbilly?" he asked with cold

41

venom. "I've heard some mighty big claims made for him."

"Yeah," drawled Calgary, before Montana could reply, "an' he'll live up to 'em, too. Give him half the practice you've had an' he'll ride Peril."

Not to be outdone in loyalty, little dreaming the price his words would exact, Kid seconded warmly: "I'll bet a month's pay Monty could ride him now."

To their utter consternation, Ranse flashed back: "I'm takin' that bet."

"Now, see here," blurted Kid, as Ranse broke into a nasty laugh, "you know I didn't mean that . . . oh, I mean he *could,* all right. But I wasn't bettin' serious, which you damned well know."

"You made a bet, an' I called you. Put up, or shut up!"

As Kid foundered helplessly, unwilling to do either, Montana said quietly: "Go on an' bet, Kid. I'll ride him."

Instantly the boys swarmed around him, vehement in their protests, and Kid Clagett loudest of all. He wouldn't help Ranse Gaines rope Montana into riding that killer for a whole year's pay. That horse had ruined one buddy for him, and he wouldn't risk another. Besides, Dan Hurn wouldn't stand for any man riding Peril.

"What makes you think so?" Ranse insisted with devilish cunning. "You all saw Hurn put him in the chute the other day."

"Yeah," came back Calgary, "an' we-all heard him raise merry Hades when you tried to put Montana on."

"Oh . . . I see." The very way Ranse lifted his light eyebrows at Montana was an insult. "It makes a difference which ox gits gored. I can git my neck broke an' be damned, but Hurn's lookin' out for his *pet.*"

The hill boy's face went white, but he gave Ranse a look that sent an electric tingle of apprehension along his spine.

"I said I'd ride him," he said, his tone unchanged.

With a snort of disbelief, Ranse shot back: "When?"

Montana's black eyes turned to the great, tawny brute wickedly watching the scene, then back to his persecutor: "Now."

Ranse laughed sarcastically. "I thought so," he sneered. "You know blamed well the boss is right over in the stable, an' would yank you off that hoss before he ever left the chute. But I'll call your bluff. Hurn's goin' to town Sunday . . . heard him tell Keno so not an hour back. Keno always drives Ma Hurn to church Sunday mornin's. So the coast will be clear with nobody to interrupt. You're right prompt at keepin' dates with Ranse's ladies" — dark blood rippled over Ranse's face — "so we'll see if you can keep a *man's* date. If you *are* a man an' not Hurn's pet, meet Yellow Peril at the chute Sunday mornin'."

Not until it was too late did they realize how cleverly Ranse had trapped Montana into that ride. How deftly he had set aside their every objection. How completely he had thought it out; and how certainly he had thrown the one taunt that would force the boy to ride.

"I'll be there," promised Montana coolly.

"Then," said Kid, sealing the awful pact, "my bet goes as she lays."

Like wildfire spread the news that Montana was going to ride the man-killer on Sunday. It burned up every other interest on the ranch, leaving black and desolating dread in every heart. Yet so clannish was the crew that not one breath of Montana's awful purpose reached Dan Hurn.

He'd have nipped that ride in the bud if it had. The boy would be killed or maimed. A miracle barring either, the only other outcome would be defeat. And defeat at this time might shake his confidence and ruin his whole future, on which Hurn was building strong. Then, too, there was the animal to consider. Yellow Peril might have to be shot to save a rider's life. Thanks to his bloody record, to the morbid curiosity of mankind in general, the man-killer was the best drawing card Hurn had.

This was Tuesday. There were five long days to wait. In them, Dan Hurn kept Montana busy, instructed him in the fine points of rodeo riding, and, by his enthusiastic interest, fanned the jealousy of Ranse Gaines beyond all control.

"Work for style," Hurn coached the hill boy. "An' keep in mind these rules. Scratch *forward* the first five jumps. Keep one hand free from start to finish, an' daylight showin' under your rein hand. You'll be judged for your mastery of a hoss, the way you scratch him, the chance you give him, an' the grace with which you do it. Don't depend on your spurs to hold you on. The bronc' fighter don't get a look in at championship rides. The judges watch the *hombre* what can reach his spurs highest on a hoss' neck."

So he tutored his apt and eager pupil, getting him ready for the opening show in Coulée City on June 15th, all unconscious of the impending clash that might bring his work and dreams to naught.

However, little else was talked of on the ranch. Whenever any two riders were together, it was a safe bet they were debating Montana's chances, or recalling, in grisly detail, Yellow Peril's victory over the two men he had slain. These battles they knew by hearsay only, for they had been fought before Dan Hurn bought the horse. But they had witnessed the third tragedy, and Yellow Peril's victim had been one of themselves.

"Who does Monty remind you of?" Kid suddenly asked of Calgary once, as they watched the boy ride.

Calgary strainedly whispered: "Bud."

Fearfully they had stared at each other then, an old nightmare reënacting itself in their minds — they saw a yellow brute buck to victory, then charge with gaping jaws and forelegs stiff, and terrible hoofs do terrible things to a prostrate rider in the dust. Just such another nervy, cool-eyed rider as Montana.

They thought of Bud now, as they saw him whenever the rodeo visited Butte — always on hand to greet them, to breathe the dust of the rodeo once more, to watch scenes in which he would never more take part, and to haunt them for weeks after by the pain and wistfulness in the eyes that watched. For Bud was chained to a wheelchair, dying daily a thousand deaths.

"Just to think," they'd say solemnly among themselves, "to be alive, an' know you couldn't ever ride again."

That was the supreme tragedy to them — then.

They prayed something might happen to make Dan Hurn call off his trip. They prayed for some calamity of nature — for it would take nothing less — to prevent the Sabbath devotions of Ma Hurn. All the time they knew this battle must be fought. Come what might, Montana must wipe out that intolerable accusation that, because of old friendship, he had some stand-in with Dan Hurn. The more success he achieved, the more jealousy he created, the more would be said. So they waited and worried.

Of them all, Montana was least concerned. He wasn't even conscious of the suspense around him. He would have been amazed to know how the week dragged to them. To him each moment was almost too full to bear, and the days had wings.

Faithfully he practiced under the guidance of Dan Hurn; found time to help Rita break in a new mount for her relay string, and to become her happy slave; to renew his old friendship with Sonny Hurn; to learn a new rope trick from Calgary, who was properly billed as "Ace of the Lariat". He never tired of watching the practice of Kid Clagett, who as a stunt rider was without a peer. And never had Montana been so happy.

Eagerly he looked ahead to Sunday — and Yellow Peril. He knew the horse was bad. *How* bad, everyone had told him. But his courage and confidence were like rock. He would prove himself to Dan Hurn and Rita. He couldn't fail. Because, as he murmured to himself one night, when sheer happiness kept him wakeful: "God's got His arm around me."

VI
"THE WRATH OF A FOOL"

On Wednesday, a new horse was delivered at Big Horn Ranch. Jeff Peters — one of the scouts Dan Hurn kept constantly on the watch for outlaw timber — had sent him, along with a letter that described him as a mighty bad actor and recited his history.

"He was caught in your neck of the woods," Hurn told Montana, when he hunted him up to try the horse out. "He's right off the Crazy Mountain range, an' he's pure dynamite, accordin' to Jeff."

Interested in this horse, thinking of how differently he might have ridden him were he still riding for the fun of it up there, Montana followed Hurn to the corral. The crew, seeing them together, surmising what was up, dropped whatever they chanced to be doing and came on the run, anxious to see the new outlaw perform.

He was already in the chute — a big, blood-red bay,

equaling Yellow Peril in size, and, seemingly, as formidable. Although he lacked the killer's vicious aspect, his widespread eyes, dilated now with hate and terror, revealed more brains. His spirit — as savagely, with tooth and hoof, he fought the barrier and the men about him — amazed them all.

"Pure dynamite is right!" Hurn was excited over this rare find. "He's goin' to give you a tussle, Monty."

As Ranse Gaines made mental note for later jealous digs, he insisted on inspecting the saddle before allowing Montana on.

"Sure of your cinch?" he asked, as they went up to do so.

"Dead sure," the boy said. "It's a new one. I made it myself. See?" With naïve pride he held up the stirrup to show it to Hurn — a hard, twisted, horsehair cinch.

"That ought to hold a buffalo," declared Hurn, satisfied.

Then he took the whistle from his pocket, and Montana cautiously lowered himself on that twitching back. The gate was kicked ajar.

A shrill cheer went up from the fence, as the wild bay plunged into the corral, rising higher in volume for one tempestuous moment, then dropped abruptly to the deep groan: "Yellow!"

For the wild horse, seeing himself surrounded by enemies, trapped in by the seven-foot fence beyond all hope of escape, gave a few dispirited cat-hops and quit cold. Nor could Montana force him to fight.

"All bluff, an' nothin' to back it," Hurn swore in disgust. "I don't savvy it a bit. Jeff wouldn't bunco me, an' he sure ought to know a bad hoss if any man does. Give him another whirl, Monty."

But nothing could arouse the bay to even one feeble buck. He stood in his tracks, his big eyes turning this way and that, in trembling, sweating terror.

"What'll I do with him?" demanded Keno, as ranch hands roped him.

"I don't care what you do" — contemptuously Dan Hurn washed his hands of the animal's fate — "so long as you git him out of my sight. There's no room in this outfit for a coward."

So the wild horse was led off in disgrace and turned into the pasture with the saddle and work stock. Often Montana saw him there, pacing the fence that was nearest the hills, his great eyes wistfully lifted to the blue heights, and always the boy's eyes smarted. Someday he would recall his own heartbreak in every detail of that ride. Someday he would ride that horse again, and then. . . . But now it was but one of the incidents that crowded his life.

Thursday passed, and Friday. Saturday was hurrying to the realm of dead time. The dreaded ordeal with Yellow Peril was but a few hours away. Feeling their responsibility for it keenly, Hurn's riders could hardly bear the strain. Repeatedly Kid tried to dissuade Montana — and let the bet forfeit. They all tried — all but Ranse.

"Don't do it, Monty," Sonny begged, intercepting him as he was leaving the cook shack that evening. "Don't let any false idea of honor get you killed . . . or crippled, like poor Bud."

To Montana — motherless, sisterless — a woman's concern was strangely sweet. He wanted to answer Sonny as she wished, but could not. Neither could he tell her why.

"They bet on me," he said soberly. "I can't throw down my friends."

Sonny's position was a cruel one. The crew counted her as one of them, and trusted their secrets with her. She couldn't betray their trust. Now she was torn between loyalty to her father and to them.

"Isn't that what you're doing," she asked earnestly, "throwing down the best friend of all?"

"Who?" he asked in wonder.

"Dad," she said. Then, with the candor he remembered of old: "You know he wouldn't let you. That's why you're waiting till he's gone. Is that acting square with Dad?"

Montana hadn't thought of it that way, and he now shamefacedly admitted that it wasn't.

"Then call it off." Sonny's violet eyes were dark with the stress of her appeal. "Don't mind what Ranse says . . . call it off."

He might have done so. But, later, when a million stars were spangling the black banner of the prairie night, he rode with a girl who paled Sonny Horn as the red flame lily paled the white anemone of his hills. This girl was a giddy, tumbleweed sort of brain. She didn't ask him to call it off, but, in her eagerness to see it, spurred him on.

"I'll be there with my ears pinned back, and my hair in a curl." Rita laughed, her dark face swept by the glamour of the starlight. "I'll be rooting for you hard."

Desiring, in her vanity, to let others know of her conquest over this man brave enough to attempt a ride on Yellow Peril, Rita took the scarlet ribbon from her hair and, bidding him dismount before her, tied it about the crown of his hat. There it would flaunt on the morrow to inflame the jealous passion of Ranse Gaines.

Inexorably, the morrow came.

Nothing occurred to call off Dan Hurn's trip, and he left for the city early. No calamity of nature intervened to save Montana, by keeping Mrs. Hurn from church. Shortly after eight, she climbed into the buckboard, and old Keno, stiffly miserable in his Sunday-go-to-meeting clothes, flourished the reins. The coast was clear, there was nobody to interrupt.

In a solemn body the cowboys went to the corral, and the girls, coming as solemnly from the ranch house, joined them. Sonny hadn't meant to come, but found herself unable to stay away.

It was a strange gathering, a strange scene, there in the brilliant sunlight of that April morn.

No banter, no friendly jostling for places at the fence. No sounds, but the stamping and snorting of horses in the outer pens, and the necessary sounds of preparations. These preparations went on swiftly, as though, having lived so long with dread, they wished an end.

Even Yellow Peril, bulking giganticly in the chute, was silent. Wise, with his awful wisdom, he knew that to fight now would be a futile waste of strength. Foolish, too, to intimidate people who already knew his power. Standing there, his muscles knotted, his wicked, bloodshot eyes watching their every move, he radiated hate as a stove does heat, suffocating, enervating them all — but Montana.

For only Montana was natural. With the girl he loved to watch his feat, wearing her colors, he could not lose. His nerves were perfectly steady as he saddled the killer, working with slow caution through the bars.

It was significant that Ranse Gaines took no part in the proceedings, but slouched against the fence, his face screened from scrutiny by his wide, shadowing sombrero, nervously pulling on a cigarette he had forgotten to light. One might have thought he held thus aloof that his hands might be clean of the consequences of that ride.

It was significant that Kid Clagett rode into the riding corral, taking up his post just inside, with rope uncoiled and made into a noose. It was even more significant when Calgary, "Ace of the Lariat", also entered, taking his stand on the other side with ready rope. Never before had it been considered necessary to have more than one man inside the fence.

With a last tug of the latigo that brought a grunt from Yellow Peril, Montana dropped the stirrup, scaled the chute, and slipped his leg over the saddle. As he settled to a firm seat, he felt the killer settle beneath him to a crouch. Then, taking off his hat, gay with Rita's ribbon, he ordered: "Let 'er buck!"

But there was one surcharged instant before they obeyed. One instant while they stared at him, the stirring picture he made on the yellow beast burning itself for all time on their minds. He was so young, so nonchalant, so eager to take his desperate chance with life. In his black eyes, glowing with excitement now, was the merest hint of a laugh that mocked their fear.

"Let 'er buck!"

Kid and Calgary stiffened in their saddles, every faculty alive. A cowboy fumblingly opened the chute gate.

Yellow Peril, with the energy of the terrible rage he had charged and stored in that long wait, doubled into a great, quivering ball, and hurled the ball that was himself into the ring. With breath suspended and heartbeats stilled, Hurn's riders saw the killer sunfish, reverse with a lightning twist, and come down with a terrific jar that snapped the boy's head back, pitching, almost in the same instant, violently forward. . . .

It happened then. So quick no eye could follow. They saw Montana hanging head down between Peril's flatted ears, still sticking like grim death to the saddle that had somehow given way. Before they could grasp the full horror of his situation, the outlaw, with the force of the thousand raging devils in him, bucked furiously back, and boy and saddle crashed to earth. Instantaneously it seemed, with the speed of hideous practice, the maddened brute reared over the prostrate form, plunging with murderous hoofs, once, twice. . . .

With a hiss, Calgary's rope snaked about those hoofs as they would have struck again. Kid's lariat encircled the corded, swollen neck. As both trained horses sat back on their haunches, the yellow fiend, with throttled, awful screams, was dragged forcibly from his prey.

Then they ran to Montana. He lay in the dust, without the slightest sign of life. A stone is heavy and the sand is weighty, but the wrath of a fool is heavier than both!

Under Sonny's directions Montana was carried to the ranch house. Kid burned up the prairie on the doctor's trail. Another cowboy raced up on Angel's Peak for Jude. Yet another galloped cityward to fetch Dan Hurn.

Ranse Gaines, skulking about the place like a lost soul, saw Rita hurrying to the corral.

"What you goin' back *there* for?" he asked hoarsely.

"My ribbon," the girl panted through her tears. "I want it . . . for a souvenir."

But out in the corral alone was one who had hurried back to seek no memento of this tragedy, but the cause. Kneeling over Montana's saddle, his homely, cheerful countenance unrecognizable from the wrath it held, Calgary muttered low and vengeful imprecations, and dangled a broken cinch.

VII
"THE SPECTER IN THE CEILING"

Dan Hurn didn't rave and storm as the boys expected and feared, but faced the disaster with fatalistic calm. The thing was done. Nothing he could say would undo it. It was just one more proof that he was hoodooed, like they said.

But cruel was his anxiety for Montana. Cruel as was his pain when he faced old Jude across the broken form of the boy so lately entrusted to his care, the shattering of his own dream, to which since the boy's amazing ride on Blackjack he had given free rein, was not less cruel. It seemed impossible that he could ever reconstruct that dream around Ranse Gaines. It only went to show how eternal is human hope that, in the end, he did.

Now as the frontier doctor came in, rolling up his sleeves, gravely eying the still form on the bed, Dan Hurd went out.

He found his crew massed outside, bareheaded in the sun, tongue-tied with dread, awaiting the doctor's verdict. Drawing Calgary aside, he demanded how it happened.

"It's by me, boss," said Calgary, meaning his inability to describe such a scene. "One minnit Monty was up there, ridin' like a house afire, an' the next . . . the cinch broke, Monty an' saddle crashed, an' that four-hoofed, yellow devil. . . ."

"What's that," Hurn said sharply. "You say the cinch broke? Why, that cinch couldn't break. I examined it yesterday an' it would have held a buffalo . . . as I told Monty at the time."

"Boss," Calgary said, mighty slow and earnest, "that cinch had help."

Hurn started. The charge was too horrible to entertain.

"That's strong talk, Cal."

"Somebody took the trouble to weaken that cinch," Calgary insisted, strangely white about the mouth. "Come on out to the saddle room, an' I'll show you."

Out there, he lifted Montana's saddle from the floor and held it while Hurn examined the frayed ends of the sturdy, hand-made cinch. If it had been deliberately weakened, Hurn decided the job had been carefully done. For it had all the earmarks of a natural break. But he had inspected it only the day before. As Calgary told him exactly how Ranse Gaines had snared the boy into that ride, Hurn's memory leaped to Ranse's face as he had seen it, black with murder, that first night, and he had a strong suspicion, too, that the cinch had had help! However, he was slow to believe a crime so hideous of one of his men.

"Cal, do the boys know this . . . about the cinch?"

"No, boss, I wanted to tell you first."

Hurn drew a deep breath of relief. "I appreciate that," he said warmly. "An', Cal, I'd sure appreciate your keepin' this under your hat."

"You ain't goin' to let Ranse git away with this!" cried the outraged cowboy. "You ain't goin' to keep him on. Not when he tried to murder Monty . . . mebbe *has* murdered him."

Hurn shrugged wearily. "What can we prove? Mebbe the cinch was cut, an' mebbe it jist broke natural. We got our suspicions, but that's all we got. All I could do with Ranse is fire him, an' I hate to do that without makin' a definite charge. We'll give him rope, Cal."

Vengeful as he was, Calgary could see that was the only thing to do. Pledged to keep the secret, he trailed morosely after Hurn back to the house.

"How did Monty act, before the . . . accident?" Hurn

swung about to ask as they neared the waiting group. "Did he show any sign of cold feet about tacklin' Peril?"

Calgary's face lit with enthusiasm. "Holy cow, no. We all had cold feet aplenty, but Monty was r'arin' to go. No show-off about it, either . . . just plain nerve. Never seen an *hombre* so sure of hisself as Monty . . . nor with half the excuse for it, what's more. Boss, as sure as I'm a foot high, he'd 'a' rode him but for that dirty, low-down, devilish trick."

This recital kindled a fire, too, in Hurn. The man who could ride Yellow Peril, could. . . . Swiftly he strode forward as the doctor stepped out on the porch.

"How is he, Doc?" Of all that group, Hurn alone had the courage to ask.

"In mighty bad shape," the physician said gravely. "Luckily there are no bones broken. But he's badly battered and bruised. And there's a head contusion or two that's got me worried."

"Anything he can't get well of?" Hurn pressed hoarsely.

"No . . . not unless some internal injury shows up."

"Doc," Hurn said tensely, as his men fled to the bunkhouse to give vent to the joy that comfort brought, "you pitch camp right here. Savvy? Don't you stir off this ranch till he's out of the woods. We've got to patch him up for the Coulée City roundup. Do your best, an' forget the cost . . . you're workin' on the future champion of the world."

The doctor stayed. A zone of quiet was described about the east wing of the house, where Montana lay, unconscious of their concern and care. But in the sick room, Jude reigned supreme.

"I'll take care of my own," he told Ma Hurn gently, when she would have taken charge. "Though I'd be obliged

55

to have you an' Sonny spell me off, now an' then."

Nor could Montana have had a better nurse. Jude's veined old hands were as gentle as a woman's, and as skilled. They had no chance to lose their cunning. For no one was ever too poor, or afflicted with a disease too loathsome, to lay claim to Jude. Small wonder that Painted Buttes range held the old hermit in reverential awe.

Jude *was* queer. There can be no denying that, nor that the world would profit were such queerness universal. There was something almost divine in his compassion for the suffering of others, his understanding of the human sins of others. No man had ever heard his voice rise in anger, or seen its shade upon his gentle face. The unremitting care with which he tended the boy was but one of the good Samaritan acts of Jude.

He had found Montana, an orphaned waif of six, given him a home and a parent's love, and been wonderfully repaid by the boy's affection. Counting on that affection to the not far-distant end, it had been a terrible wrench to him when Montana chose a life so far removed from his, and terrible must have been the pain he felt now, seeing what that life had already done to him. But, whatever his thoughts, they never crossed his lips.

Hours he sat by the bedside, his eyes bent on the boy's still face, his lips moving in silent prayer. Or, his snowy head bent over the Book he loved, he sought with faltering finger some word of comfort now.

But, as it happened, Jude was not with Montana when he struggled back to consciousness through a hell of pain. He opened his eyes and saw, above, the beamed ceiling of the room, and his eyes dilated in horror, and he shrank back in a very frenzy of fear. For, in his fevered state, that ceiling became the last thing his waking eyes had seen, was fever changed into a sentient thing, an awful being — the screaming yellow beast that reared and struck.

In his helplessness, pain-chained, unable to escape those killing hoofs, he screamed in mortal terror. Into the black frenzy of his fear came a voice that held the brute, that stayed those hoofs. It was a woman's voice, soothing as the wind that sang through the deep pines of his hills, and he knew, somehow, that it belonged to Sonny Hurn.

"It's all right, Monty," she assured him.

Now he thought of cool, fern-banked mountain rills, and, so thinking, he fell asleep.

"Doc," Hurn said gravely when he heard, "I've had years of practice, too, with just such men an' injuries. It's an internal injury of another kind I fear."

But the doctor scouted that with a vehemence that relieved him. "It's only natural. He's sustained a bad shock to his nerves. He'll come out of it, if you give him time."

Two days went by — two days of pain, of fitful sleep and hideous wakings when even old Jude, holding water to his lips, would change into the fearful demon in the ceiling, and in his delirium he would cry out for Sonny, whose voice alone had power to hold back the brute. To Sonny only, when his brain was clear and the beams assumed and kept their true proportions, could he confide his terror and the horrors he had seen. From her quiet understanding of this chimera, he drew strength.

VIII
"UP AGAIN"

But, growing stronger, Montana turned petulantly from Sonny Hurn. She evoked the peace and quiet of the old life he had renounced. It was the glamour of the new life he craved — the girl who personified the rodeo to him. Yet, days passed and Rita never came.

"What's all the outfit doin'?" he asked wistfully of Sonny, when again she came to sit by him when Jude was at table, and he prayed that she would mention Rita, of whom pride and shyness made it difficult to ask.

"Resting, Monty." Sonny ignored his pleading look. "That big bay Jeff sent broke out and went back to the hills, taking some of the saddle horses with him. The boys have put in several days' hard work, rounding them up."

He asked her if they got the bay. When she told him no, he was glad, remembering the homesick way the horse had watched the hills. Then, when longing beat down diffidence and pride: "What's Rita doin'? They've all been in to see me . . . all but Reet."

"She's gone for a ride," Sonny answered, but did not add that it was with Ranse. "She asks about you, Monty. But she says sick rooms make her nervous and blue."

"Then she mustn't come . . . ever!" cried the boy, with an earnestness that brought tears to Sonny's eyes.

He was silent for moments then, his eyes passing slowly over the pleasant room with its simple, cozy furnishings, and to the girl again. She sat in a low chair beside the open casement, her sweet face bent over some needlework, and the dancing sunbeams making a nimbus about her rich, bronze hair.

"They don't make *you* nervous, Sonny . . . sick folks, I mean?"

She looked up at that abrupt query, her work dropping to her lap. "Bless you, no." She laughed. "I love them. I always did."

"Yeah, you did." He smiled reminiscently. "I mind once

when we were kids I stubbed my toe, an' you cried when the blood came. But you tore up your little petticoat an' bandaged it, an' you fussed over me for an hour after. You ain't changed much since then."

"I haven't had a chance," Sonny said hurriedly, several shades pinker than before. "Dad's been in this business ever since I can remember, and I can't recall a season when we haven't had at least one rider in this room getting well of a broken arm, or collar bone, or worse. So, as Mother says, I've kept my hand in nursing."

Again he was silent, digesting this. A pretty girl like Sonny — and she was awfully pretty in this gingham dress, violet, like her eyes — confined to a sick room, waiting on banged-up riders.

"It's a shame," he burst out suddenly, "that you have to take care of me! You tried your best to keep me off Peril."

Could he be reproaching that other girl — the one who spurred him on, who, having won her wish, could not risk nervousness by a visit? No, the boy's first love was much too deep for that.

One day soon after, when for the moment he was quite alone, he woke from a doze to see her at his bedside — more beautiful than he had ever dreamed. His heart set up in a prodigious pounding at sight of the present she had brought. For her arms were full of long-stemmed, scarlet, flame lilies, to which he had often likened her. Lilies, as Montana knew, not native to the plains, but found only in the dry woods of his hills. At this early season, long sought to find so many.

"You . . . you went clean up there" — his dark eyes were incredulous with joy — "to fetch me these."

Rita denied that smilingly. "Ranse got them. I told him they were my favorite flower, and he was away all afternoon hunting them for me. But" — she was touched by the pain on the boy's white face — "I told him that, Monty, because I wanted them for you."

For that thought of him, he endured them, although sight of the exquisite vermilion flowers made him sick. Sick with jealousy, that Ranse had meant them for the girl he loved.

"Tell me," he cried huskily, seizing her hand, "which do you like best . . . me, or Ranse?"

But no entreaty could make Rita answer.

Now Montana was in a very agony of impatience to be up and doing. While he lay here, Ranse was stealing Rita from him. He grew haggard with the torment of his thoughts, even as his body healed.

"Son," tremulously said observant old Jude one day, "jealousy is as cruel as the grave."

"Don't I know it," Montana groaned. "But I can't help it. I've heard you read how many waters couldn't quench love, or the floods drown it. You can't help bein' jealous, no more'n you can help lovin'."

Yet he didn't know that the jealousy of another man had almost meant the grave for him. He learned that the next day, inadvertently, from Sonny Hurn.

"Jude says pride goes before a fall," he told her, with something like his old-time grin. "Well, I sure was proud before mine. I got to thinkin' I was some tallow, an' it took only Yellow Peril about three jumps to. . . ."

"It wasn't your fault," broke in Sonny warmly. "It's no slam on your riding that the cinch broke."

She was startled by the strange way his eyes burned on her, by the way he struggled up and stared at her, and the intensity of his query: "You say the . . . cinch . . . broke?"

She nodded. But she couldn't convince him, and, bringing the cinch from the saddle room, she placed it in his trembling hands that he might know it was for a mechanical reason and through no fault of his own that the ride had failed.

But its effect was not what she hoped. Long the boy stared at the broken ends, literally freezing up. No strain could have parted that cinch. It was made of fresh, hand-picked hair, and cable was not stronger. He had made it especially for his try-out with Hurn. He could see exactly what had been done, and, looking back, knew to a certainty who had done it. Yet he said nothing about it to Jude, Dan Hurn, or anyone else.

Still water runs deep, and deep ran the current of Montana's resolve for vengeance. So deep, that only once or twice in its not lengthy course did it appear in morbid flashes on the surface. For he was the mountain type that dams the deeper emotions, till, restrainable no longer, the pent-up, devastating flood burst forth. He was thrice as dangerous for that same restraint. Ranse had him down now. But — someday he'd be up.

He was up and about by the middle of May, chumming with Calgary and Kid, riding with Rita, seemingly none the worse for his encounter with Yellow Peril. Search as Dan Hurn did, in his anxiety, for a difference, he could see none, unless it was his deliberate avoidance of the stockade that held the killer. But if Montana's delirious terror was natural, Hurn reasoned, this was even more so.

That there was a difference was forcefully revealed to the boy himself one afternoon.

He, Calgary, and Kid were perched on the high log that spanned the gate posts when ranch hands swung the gate under them, to turn the rodeo outlaws out to pasture for the night. The horses were piling up beneath them, snorting, rearing, fighting through the exit, wilder than ever, now that they sensed freedom of a sort, when Kid, with a piercing yell, cried — "Follow your leader!" — and jumped from the log to the bare back of one of the plunging horses.

While Montana's heart stood still with sudden horror, Calgary with the same yell dropped to the back of another.

In less time than it takes to tell, both horses had bucked clear, and both cowboys were rolling in the dust. As they got up, and came back grinning, Montana realized that he was shaking all over — felt sick. Why? This was just another of the daredevil stunts they pulled off daily, that he used to do himself, had thought was fun. What was the matter with him? Why did it seem foolish, wicked, to take chances like that?

"Feelin' fit, Monty?" Dan Hurn stood below him.

"Yeah," said the boy, getting down.

"That's fine," Hurn approved eagerly. "I don't want to put you in the harness too quick . . . but the Coulée City date is creepin' up. Think you can ride tomorrow?"

The boy said — "Sure." — although the thought raced through his brain that he'd be flirting with death himself tomorrow.

That night he couldn't sleep. His mind persisted in going through all the motions of riding a bucking horse. He felt the angry swelling of the animal beneath him, as he settled in the saddle and gripped the reins. He fancied himself swaying back, in the one position that makes a rider's balance possible on a pitching mount, and leaves the legs free to sweep the horse from neck to flank in that spectacular performance known as scratching.

He envisioned the launching of so many hundred pounds

of infuriated horseflesh from chute to corral, felt the terrible, racking heaves, then — the sensation of emptiness beneath him, the sickening sense of falling, the stunning jar, and, as cold fear numbed his brain, he saw the great, tawny killer upreared to strike.

Always he felt and envisioned that. Try as he might to terminate these mental rides in success to the rider, he could not. Always in the midst of that heaving he felt himself thrown, and saw that awful specter.

Once in the saddle, he thought surely, *I'll git my ol' grip back.*

But would he ever ride with the old disregard of consequences, with the iron nerve that had been his most outstanding trait — which was the greatest asset a rodeo rider can have?

Wondering that kept Dan Hurn wakeful, too.

IX
"AFRAID"

Jude was still at Big Horn Ranch. God alone knew why he stayed. For he yearned for home, as only age can yearn for its own rooftree, however humble, or however hospitable the one where it is guest. Every night he promised himself to go home next day, yet lingered on. When word reached Angel's Peak that Montana had been hurt, he had called in a neighbor's boy to tend his flock. Now he mistrusted the faithfulness of that boy's care, and was, to quote Dan Hurn, "restless as a witch."

But this morning, lying beside Montana in the bunk they shared, the longing for the green hills seemed too strong to resist. He'd see the boy ride today, then he'd go home.

As the forenoon wore on, Jude was surprised and pleased at the interest all evinced in Montana's return to work, giving his first ride the status of an event, rather than mere routine. For the boy's popularity, his courage in attempting to ride Yellow Peril, his defeat for an accidental cause, and his subsequent injury had intensified their first interest in him and accounted for the enthusiasm with which Hurn's outfit greeted him at the corral.

"How about Tar Baby for a starter?" suggested Hurn, who was obviously under a strain.

The boy nodded indifferently and said: "Any."

For *his* whole interest, as Jude noted, was in Rita Sills. As usual the girl had monopolized him, was enmeshing him more firmly in the exotic pattern of her spell. The old man saw Ranse Gaines staring at them, sullen-eyed. He knew what was in his heart, and vast uneasiness came over him. But what could he do? Who could cope with the first white flame of love?

Then Montana, proudly escorted by Calgary and Kid, went up to the chute where Tar Baby raged. The boy's saddle, with its brand-new cinch, was fastened on. This horse — a twisty bucker, who insured a spectacular show at no particular cost to the rider — had been ridden by Montana once before, and aroused no emotion in him now. It was all mechanical — this part.

Mechanically he eased into the saddle, felt the angry swell beneath him, and his breath came hard and fast, for suddenly all things were real. But he forced a smile to his lips, jerked the blindfold from Tar Baby's eyes, and swayed back. The gate swung on the instant, and he was catapulted into the corral. Cheers beat in his ears with his own heart-throbs, as the outlaw went into the familiar racking bucks he'd envisioned. Then, like a light blown out, confidence wavered, and dizzying nausea assailed him.

Something had given way. The saddle was slipping — he was falling. Why did they cheer? He was falling. . . . The reeling corral, the taut watchers faded, and he saw himself *fallen*, helpless, and over him, not Tar Baby, but the yellow killer with striking hoofs and open jaws. He knew it was imagination only, but he could not force it from his mind. More vivid the specter grew, wave after wave of horror swept him, weakened him, and, resistless to the next great heave, *he fell!*

Shame stung him back to reality, as he struggled up, dazed by the jar, strangled, blinded by the dust of the corral. The boys were running to him.

"What a spill!" joked Calgary, seeing his shame. "It happens in the best-regulated families, pal."

But that didn't lessen his agony. It wasn't the cinch *this* time. Something had broken, all right. To his soul's despair, Montana knew what had.

Going back to the fence, he saw on Hurn's face such a look as a man, thirst crazed, might cast on the cup that is dashed from his fevered lips. Yet that didn't lash the boy's raw and sensitive spirit as much as the pity with which Hurn said: "Reckon we put you on too soon."

Easier to bear was Ranse Gaines's sneer: "A flash in the pan. An' they set *him* up for a star."

"He is . . . a *falling* star." Rita giggled.

The boy, hearing, stumbled blindly from the scene. Rita knew. She despised him. Dan Hurn knew.

"A flash in the pan," he moaned to Jude, when the old man found him in the bunkhouse later, sitting on his bunk, with his burning face buried in his palms. "Well . . . I'm done. I'm through."

Sharing his misery to the last dull pang, Jude put his arm

around him, saying kindly: "You're afraid, son."

"No," the boy shrank from the truth. "Something jist came over me. . . ."

"Fear," defined Jude gently. "You didn't know what it means to fear a horse, son, but you've learned. Yellow Peril put the fear of a horse in you."

"I saw him," Montana shuddered, "makin' for me, an' I jist went limp. I see him in my dreams, Jude . . . an' I git numb."

"I know, son," quavered the old man earnestly. "But you got no call to fear Yellow Peril . . . or any horse. For God gave man domination over the birds of the air, the fish of the sea, and over every beast of earth."

The boy cried, rising: "I'll try again!"

His reappearance at the corral, where training was going on as usual, created quite a stir. Loyal as they were, not one of Hurn's riders expected Montana to be a rider again. He had sustained the most fatal of all injuries — a broken nerve. Remembering what his nerves had been made it seem doubly cruel. They were surprised when he stepped up and asked Hurn for another horse.

"Any preference?" Hurn was eager, for hope died hard. He gave him See-Saw, when he waived a choice.

Lost his nerve — Montana? Did it not take courage of no mean order to mount again and face that line-up of pitying faces, feeling as he did? To face Ranse Gaines, who wanted to see him fail? To face the girl he loved and risk total heartbreak by her laugh? To face Dan Hurn, who believed in him, had given him his chance? And Jude whose eyes were fixed sorrowfully and prayerfully upon him, and who shared his shame?

Yet he faced them. On one of the wildest horses in Dan Hurn's string. There was a grim, set smile on his lips that made their hearts go out to him.

Again he sat a pitching mount in the corral. Again, fight desperately as he did, came that awful vision, weakening him, paralyzing him, and — again he was thrown. Oh, he couldn't believe it. He couldn't believe in his own suffering.

"I'm done," he moaned, once more in the sanctuary of the bunkhouse. "The show'll go on the road without me. I wish to God Peril had killed me. I'm done . . . an' there ain't no help."

Again old Jude was there to comfort. "There *is* help," he said tremulously. "Help, if you'll take it, son."

"I'll take it!" cried the tormented youth.

The old man got out the Book that was his friend, philosopher, and guide, and with a gnarled old finger pointing to the words, he read: " 'And the fear of you shall be upon every beast of earth . . . into your hand are they delivered'."

By a desperate effort the boy pulled himself together. For Jude's sake, he'd try again. "If Dan Hurn will let me."

Dan Hurn let him, although he felt it would be kinder not to. The riders stayed, although it was painful to them, and they felt it would be a kindness to Montana to disperse.

All stayed for this ride — the last Montana would ever make in that corral. They, who had seen his proudest moments, were to witness his supreme humiliation and defeat.

Once more he was in the saddle. Once more Jude prayerfully watched. Once more an outlaw horse and a slim young rider crashed into the ring. Once more, in the first spasm of bucking, Jude saw Montana's form go slack, and the seal of horror stamp itself upon his face. It came to Jude as an inspiration then — to shock the boy, make him forget that other shock.

Intent on Montana, none saw the old man leap inside the fence. None saw him till he was beside the fighting horse and set-faced rider, presenting a figure so eerie in that setting, with white locks flying, bony arms upflung, his weathered face aflame with wrath and scorn, that they stared at him as at an apparition. Superstitious awe ran through old Jude as, pat to his lips, as always in a crisis, leaped a phrase from the Book he loved, delivered in a voice so strange, ringing so loud above the tattoo of hoof beats, that it broke down the ice wall of Montana's horror: " 'When your fear cometh, I will mock'!"

Stronger than any other shock to Montana was the shock of gentle old Jude in wrath, more horrible than any other horror, that of Jude's mockery. The specter of Yellow Peril receded, and. . . .

Kid and Calgary ecstatically hugged each other, emitting whoop on whoop. Tears of joy rained down Sonny's cheeks. Rita's eyes were luminous. Ranse Gaines glowered. A mighty load was lifted from Dan Hurn's soul. Old Jude wept, with Sonny, tears of joy — and remorse.

For suddenly Montana was riding. Not mechanically, as one who awaits defeat, but beautifully, and with all his old-time grace and verve.

A few seconds only he rode thus, the vision of Jude growing dimmer, numbing paralysis claiming him, as the old vision of the yellow fiend came back. A heave, a human scream. . . . And he was creeping, stunned and bleeding, out of the corral dust.

Out of the welter of blood and dust and sweat, to which he had ridden in so much eagerness and hope, had come, not the great end the hill boy sought, but the end of hope. For this was the end. He could stay no longer, no longer bear the crushing shame, no longer make a spectacle of himself before the girl he loved — a spectacle that had aroused even Jude's disgust. Just to get away, to hide —

hide. Break out in the night and run — like Dynamite, the wild horse that had turned out yellow.

"There's no room in this outfit for a coward," Dan Hurn had said.

Then there was no room for him.

That night, while the bunkhouse lay deep in its first sleep, Montana arose, so silently that Jude, who had denied the call of the hills to stay with him now, had no knowledge of his moving. Then, with feverish haste he dressed. Not in the clothes that Dan Hurn had given him, but in the patched old shirt, the tattered blue jeans, the battered hat, that he had worn down from the hills.

He had thought himself poor when he came, but he had been rich — rich in joy, hope, and courage. All these he was leaving at Big Horn Ranch. From it, he was taking nothing but bitter memories and the determination to have revenge.

For a moment, before leaving, he bent over the bunk where Kid and Calgary lay. Long, by the pale moonlight, he looked into their sleeping faces, and his lips quivered in a soundless: "Good bye."

But passing the bunk where Ranse Gaines slept, his loose mouth open, his yellow hair wild about his face, Montana paused, and on the heaving blanket over Ranse's breast laid one half of the broken cinch.

"So you'll know," he muttered harshly, "that I won't forget." Placing the other half inside his shirt, he passed outside.

It was no trick for him to find his saddle in the dark, or to summon his mustang by a whistle to the gate. Then he was mounted and on the drive. As he passed the ranch house, he halted and looked up at the dark window that marked Rita's room.

"A fallin' star," was his strangled cry, as the hot tears came at last. "They say . . . when you . . . see one . . . it's a sign somebody . . . died. I died . . . today. An' I went . . . to hell."

X
"DYNAMITE"

Oh, the hell of that night flight when blinded by tears, choked by sobs, Montana took his broken pride, his broken nerves, away from Big Horn Ranch. Where away, he neither knew nor cared. Yet, instinctively as a wild thing seeking to bear alone his mortal hurt, his flight lay toward the hills. The faithful mountains lifted thick, impenetrable walls between the tortured boy and the things that tortured, but he did not know. The night birds and the whispering night wind in the forest welcomed him back, but he did not hear. The healing stillness of the solitudes beat on his quivering spirit, but he did not feel.

While still the dark lay thick about him, he came to the cabin on Angel's Peak, and knew he could not stay. It was his home by the bounty of old Jude only. He had disgraced Jude, and it was not home. He took down his rifle from the wall, moving so soundlessly that the boy who slept there did not hear. Reluctantly he took a little — a very little — flour and salt. With these things, necessary to maintain life, he resumed his flight.

Hill after hill he crossed, and the deep gorges that lay between. When dawn grayed the sky, and weariness made his mustang falter, he drew rein, in the very heart of the wild.

Hobbling his horse that it might not stray, he threw himself prone on the soft earth, his face pillowed in his arms, and gave way to the feelings that were tearing him to pieces. He wore himself out with grief, and, succumbing then to the spell of the solitudes, he slept — so soundly, that no harrowing dream intruded, so long, that the new day was waning when he waked.

Struggling up, he looked about him, and even in his misery he thrilled.

On every side rose the mountains with their murmurous forests. The little valley in which he lay seemed, in the ruby haze of sunset, to be the very dwelling place of peace. A stream ran through it, chuckling in its meanderings, dimpling, flashing over cool, mossy stones. Across the stream was an old log cabin, with door hospitably ajar. Beyond the cabin, at the head of the valley, was a large log corral.

"Some stockman built it," he conjectured, as he explored the place, "when feed was scarce on the plains, an' he was holdin' a herd up here."

Although long abandoned, it did not have that melancholy look of desertion such places usually wear. Wild roses nodded companionably in the cabin window, and wild morning glory vines clambered hilariously through the chinks.

"A little bit of heaven," whispered Montana, beautystruck. "I wouldn't leave it . . . ever, if it was mine."

As days passed, to keep out the poisoned shafts of memory, he filled his mind with thoughts of what he'd do if this little bit of heaven were his own. It could be his, if he wanted it, for all this section was government land and open to homestead entry. So, with a complete sense of possession he made his plans.

He'd get a start of cattle and run them in the hills. He'd drain that swamp where the tules were, and put all the bottomland in hay for winter feed. He'd fence in the south slopes, and make a pasture for Jude's flock. He'd build another room on the cabin for Jude. . . .

But I can't plan for Jude this time, he'd remember, his dark eyes strained with pain. *He don't want no more truck with me. Jude mocked me.*

But he had to think of something else, or he'd go loco. For the days were long — and it took such a little of each to kill a pheasant or rabbit and broil it on his lonely fire, leaving the rest a dead weight on his hands — and when idle he couldn't help but think.

So he went on planning. Because he must have someone he loved to weave his daydreams around, he dreamed he'd married Rita and brought her here. But by no flight of imagination could he "dream" her over the cabin sill. Rita hated the hills — she'd told him that in their first talk. She had to have new towns, new crowds, new thrills.

While he tried to win her over in his fancy, a girl entered the cabin and took up her abode there as by natural right. A girl who made you think of mountain rills and silent places, who was the same good comrade in sickness as in health. A girl who didn't laugh when an *hombre*'s heart was breaking. A girl — with violet eyes.

Oftenest in his fancy, Montana saw her, dressed in gingham of violet hue, sitting in a low chair by the window, with the sunbeams making a halo of her hair. Strangely, although, she had the soul and likeness of Sonny Hurn, he called her Rita in his heart.

To make the cabin fit for her and give substance to his dreams, to keep off black reality that fought always at the portals of his mind, he made a broom of pine boughs and swept the cabin clean. He reinforced the corral and hidden wings, working with primitive tools he'd made. Then, to give the place an occupied look, he turned the mustang in.

Thus the days dragged by, with him living in the present, his mind locked to the past, and with no thought of what he'd do when this game had played itself out.

There were, of course, dreadful moments when his longing for Calgary and Kid, the old banter, excitement, swirl of ropes and dust were too strong to be denied. There were dreadful moments when the highlights of his life at Big Horn would come back — the day when he'd handed the sombrero to Ranse along with his promise never to forget; the star-spangled night when Rita gave him the ribbon from her hair; the crushing, unforgettable moment when, helpless before the hideous specter of Yellow Peril, he had heard Jude's voice in wrath.

But, gradually, these moments became less frequent, and frequently his whole being sang in tune with the spirit of the wild. He knew then how he'd missed this freedom, this "lift" of altitude, this brooding peace, even in his happiest days down there. The hills had always been home to him. Now they were more than ever home. They sheltered, strengthened, fed him now — *now* — when he was a coward.

"A hillbilly," he'd call himself at such times with real pride. "I'll stick by them, too . . . I'll stay." But no — he couldn't stay. He had to go back — not to ride, for he couldn't ride, but. . . . His fingers would close convulsively about his half of the broken cinch.

In these moments of deep revulsion, he would think of how he'd failed Dan Hurn who had banked on him; how he'd failed himself; think of that shameful day when he'd tried and tried to ride, knowing beforehand he could not; think with burning heart of Rita's laugh — nor blame her. It was no wonder that she laughed — that Jude mocked.

Then he'd think of the rodeo showing in Coulée City. Of

Ranse making the big ride, while he skulked like a coyote here. Even his thwarted ambition would rise to crucify him, by raking up all that might have been.

"Oh, God!" he cried one twilight, when reality had driven the dream girl from his side. "If you ain't gone back on me, too . . . help me. Fix it so I can go back."

And, miraculously, a way was pointed.

Riding in the valley one afternoon, more than two weeks after his flight, one week from the date of the opening show, Montana's keen eyes picked up a moving cluster of dots far up the mountainside — a band of grazing horses.

"Wild ones," he whispered, tingling to an old familiar thrill. Wild mustangs, such as he used to trap and ride — for fun; on which he had qualified himself to ride for Hurn — before he'd seen Yellow Peril and learned the meaning of fear, before he'd forgotten how to ride. Suddenly came a thought that took his breath, set his heart hammering, made his dark, upflung face glow, rapt.

Here, alone in the wilds, he had learned to ride. Here in his natural element, with no one to pity or scorn, he might learn again. If he were killed here, what did it matter? Wasn't he dead now — the same as dead? He'd rather be dead than not be in Coulée City with the rest. If only he could learn to ride, ride for the championship, be a man again — come back.

Lifted out of his hopelessness by even this pallid hope, he sent his mustang circling the mountain. Riding against the wind so that his scent would not carry and warn the band, he rounded a ledge and saw them feeding not a hundred yards away. He stopped, staring, surprise tearing from his lips the amazed cry: "Dynamite!"

For there, before his eyes, head lifted in a startled poise

74

for flight, was the great bay Hurn had despised because he was a coward. The horse who had failed Hurn, as he had failed him, and who had fled to the hills, even as he had fled.

Now as the bay, with a piercing blast, wheeled and pounded over the slope with the band after, Montana recklessly spurred behind. Over treacherous slide, fissure, and bluff he galloped, his eyes straining on the ruddy-coated leader of the band.

But why tell of that chase, when the thing that counted was the miracle that came after? By an hour's desperate riding in and out of the mountain pockets; by the exercise of a lifetime's knowledge of wild horse ways, which nothing could take from him, Montana herded them down into the valley, into the mouth of the funneling corral wings, concealed by leafy brush, and down to the narrow neck that was the gate of the log corral.

Here they reared back, screaming, but Montana barred their way, and, shrieking like a madman, madly waving his hat from side to side, he drove them in. Then, flinging himself from the saddle, he slammed the corral bars in place, and leaned against them, breathing hard.

But not for long. He had only a week to learn what he had once spent years in learning. He'd begin now — begin on Dynamite. Then shame seared him. The bay was yellow. He'd buck for a time or two and quit. Naturally he would pick him. Because *he* was yellow, too, and the horse was just about his size.

But not even shame swerved him from his purpose. Taking his rope, he climbed the corral, waited for the plunging, snorting mass of horseflesh to untangle and, when the bay emerged, dropped the noose about his head. Having been broken to the halter at Big Horn Ranch, the horse did not fight the rope long. Nor did Montana experience much trouble in hazing him outside the gate, and snubbing him hard and fast to one of the upright logs of the corral.

But when, keeping a grim hold on the rope, he heaved his saddle on the quivering back, the stallion went wild. Savagely, with tooth and hoof, he fought that cinching, as he had fought the men at the Big Horn chute.

"All bluff an' nothin' to back it!" Dan Hurn had said then.

"Me an' you . . . both!" Montana told the wild horse now.

Then his foot was in the stirrup and he was in the saddle, and the stallion's mighty muscles writhed beneath him into knots. Once he loosed the snub rope, it was between the horse and him. No "pick-up" here, on the alert to rope and hold the beast when the old vision numbed him and he fell. No possible outside help.

With lips compressed to a fighting line, Montana loosed the rope.

Hissingly it ripped out of its coils about the post. With a bawl that rang fearfully down the valley, the bay reared, gigantic, beating the air with great fore hoofs. Coming down almost at once, he leaped into a tremendous, spine-snapping buck, and then — when Montana thought the battle over — began to fight.

For this was no coward who sweated terror and couldn't be made to fight. Here, with no net of fences between himself and freedom, with but one adversary, and a fighting chance — he fought.

A demon, fiery of form and spirit, with mane, tail, and snub rope flying wildly, he lashed his maniacal course straight down the valley, doubling back, in lightning flashes, as he sunfished, spun, and pitched, to strike at the boy's legs with frightful jaws.

Montana had ridden many an outlaw, yet this one combined the worst features of them all. Moments of it, and the terrible jars beat blood into his eyes and ears, sent it trickling from his nostrils, made of his body one gnawing ache, one killing pain.

Past the cabin, through the cottonwood grove, down on the creek flat, the desperate battle waged. Ruthless past all telling, past all enduring. Oh, the pity of it, that no one was there to see. Yet, through it all, Montana had the hazy, crazy notion that the girl was there, white with horror, screaming that she could not bear it — that it must stop.

It would stop — soon. For his little bit of heaven swam in a mist of red, was turning black — just as he saw, on his left, the waving tules of the swamp. Instinctively he drove his spur in the buckling shoulder away from it, struck repeatedly, savagely, with the last of his strength, in an effort to force the stallion into the swamp, as he had forced Blackjack to land beside Ranse Gaines's hat, and. . . .

The black world heaved and rocked and seemed to split amain. The tules closed around him. Dimly, as in another world, he knew that he was down there with Dynamite, threshing in the ooze. As from another world and other lips, he heard his faint, weird laughter, as again he was menaced by thrashing hoofs.

XI
"THE HOODOO SCORES AGAIN"

In the meanwhile, things hummed increasingly at Big Horn Ranch. The time was fast approaching when Hurn's

Wild West Show would go on the road. The grain-fed outlaws, heady, conceited from many victorious conflicts, were ready to pit their strength against the strongest pair of legs that ever cowboy grew. The riders, too, were on edge and in perfect trim. With advance reports predicting a "large" season, the wildest enthusiasm should have prevailed. But a cloud of gloom hung over the ranch. They couldn't forget Montana. Where was he? Why had he gone? They wondered and worried.

"I done it," old Jude moaned that first morning, so frail and feeble that he seemed literally to break before their eyes. "I run him off. I meant to help him . . . and I drove him off from me."

"We all make mistakes," Dan Hurn said, remorsefully thinking that his own mistake in rushing the boy back to work had been the biggest.

Then Jude had hurried up to Angel's Peak, only to find that Montana had been there and gone.

"I'm stayin' there till he comes home," he quavered to Dan Hurn, when anxiety had torn the showman from the thousand-and-one details demanding his attention. "He will come home, won't he, Dan? He'll remember I'm old, won't he, and make allowances for me? You think he'll come home?" He searched Hurn's face with pathetic earnestness for an answer.

"He'll come home." Hurn couldn't deny that look. "An' the minute he does, Jude, bring me word."

The old man promised.

But days slipped by and no word came from Montana, nothing to show that he even lived.

"He wasn't like us" — Kid worried, when Calgary squatted down by his side in a breathing spell — "things struck deep with Monty. Cal, you struck deep with Monty.

78

Cal, you don't reckon he'd . . . ?" He couldn't complete the thought, but Calgary knew.

"Nope," he said firmly, "he ain't done that. For he would be yellow then . . . an' Monty ain't."

But they wished they could see him, could tell him that they didn't think the less of him for falling, but respected him more for his game tries. He wasn't the first man to have his nerve shattered by a fiend like Yellow Peril, nor would he be the last. They wanted to tell him that it wasn't any disgrace, any reason to. . . .

"He didn't run from us . . . but from Jude," Kid decided with a sort of awe. "An' if I'd 'a' been Monty, I'd be runnin' yet. It was enough to make any *hombre* fall off his hoss . . . to have soft-spoken ol' Jude jump on him like . . . like. . . ."

"Like he was callin' out the thunder an' lightnin'," suggested Calgary in the same sort of awe. And Kid said yes.

Then they were silent, watching the colorful whirlwind before them, and thinking how Bud's tragedy had been a mercy compared to this. To be alive and not able to ride wasn't anywhere near so awful as to be physically able to ride, and have some quirk of the brain forbid.

"Waal," concluded Kid, as they rose, "Monty's loss is Ranse's gain."

"Which if he ever crows to me about," vowed Calgary tensely, "I'll plumb massacre him."

Obedient to Hurn's wishes, the cowboy had told no one of their suspicions concerning the broken cinch. But whenever he thought of it — and it was no suspicion, far as Calgary was concerned — he could hardly keep his hands off Ranse Gaines. He was, in fact, so openly and consistently pugnacious toward him that Dan Hurn took him to task.

"Cool down, Cal," he warned one day. "You know

Ranse is our one chance to break that hoodoo. I can't have you messin' him up at this stage of the game."

Calgary's jaw set stubbornly. "The only reason I ain't made a mess of him," he retorted, "is because I'm prayin' Monty'll come back an' do it himself."

Hurn was patient with him, for he understood, even shared his feelings in no small degree. He'd seen many a promising rider flunk, but never one whose flunking affected him as Montana's had. Yet he couldn't bring himself to believe that Ranse was responsible for it. If he was. . . .

"I've allus noticed, Cal," he said solemnly, "that an *hombre* gets just about what he gives in this world."

"Mebbe," Calgary snorted, "but the rule ain't workin' with Ranse."

Nor did it seem to be. For with Montana out of the way, the big, blond braggart had resumed the place of stellar importance in Hurn's outfit, was again, as the boys resentfully put it, "the whole show". Yet it is safe to say that not Calgary or Kid thought oftener of Montana than Ranse did.

For he had found Montana's pregnant message — that piece of broken cinch — and had interpreted it in the way Montana meant. It was a tribute to the boy how deeply he took that threat to heart. It developed in him a strange nervousness about his riding gear, so that he never mounted a bucking horse without first going over his equipment microscopically, as if fearful that it had been tampered with. And he was never in the saddle but he feared such damage had been done and overlooked. Impossible for Ranse Gaines to conceive the strange way in which the hill boy would pay him back.

In love, as in the saddle, now that his rival was gone, Ranse had a clear field. He monopolized Rita as he had before Montana's coming, was her shadow — but not her slave. For he assumed a masterful way with her that Rita liked. Constantly they were together.

"Girl, you've got me plumb hobbled an' tied to a post," he whispered huskily, as they stood in a group watching Calgary perform miracles with his rope.

Rita flashed back — "Then I've got you where I want you." — and laughingly retreated to the other girls before his ardent advance.

Rita was the same thrill-obsessed, irresponsible, irresistible coquette as when she'd spurred Montana to his ruin. Did she ever think of him? Did she share their worry? It wasn't likely, for with Rita's kind, out of sight was out of mind.

But there was one who thought of him, one who could imagine the hell of what he was going through. Many times each day, Sonny's eyes would lift to the blue-misted hills, and always the tears would come. She felt sure that he was there, and she was glad.

"He didn't belong here," she told her father at dinner, when he was fretting about the accident.

"If ever there was one *hombre* what did belong in a rodeo," Dan Hurn said earnestly, "it was Montana, afore he was hurt. I wish to heaven I had him back like he was then."

"I wasn't thinking of his riding," Sonny mused thoughtfully, dallying with her dessert.

"What was you thinkin', honey?" Hurn was curious.

"Oh . . . I don't know. I'd hate to see him make a profession of it . . . that's all. I've noticed that the men who follow it aren't much good for anything else. It would spoil him for living . . . for this isn't living, Dad, this rushing from town to town, always in a mob, stifle, and din. It would suffocate Montana, kill all that's genuine in him. . . ." She paused in confusion, realizing the warmth of her tone. "Whatever you say, Dad," — her eyes were defiant — "this life's not real."

Hurn grinned ruefully. "Ain't you takin' some mean digs at your ol' dad's callin'?" he teased. "If rodeo life ain't real, what is it?"

"It's . . . like this," Sonny said seriously, lifting a bit of meringue on her spoon, "all fluff and froth. Good for a taste, exciting, but it doesn't nourish or satisfy. You've got to dig deep under to get the real thing."

Hurn stared at her, open-mouthed. Later he would give that speech the consideration it deserved, but then he was only capable of a loud and fervent: "Waal, I'll be danged!"

He was almost as restless these last days as the yellow killer pacing the pen out there. He tried hard not to build his hope too high, although Ranse had taken hold of his work and was developing in a way that justified it. He kept tabs on the men who would fight their way up through the preliminaries that season. Most of the old riders he knew, and he thought Ranse had a chance. But, lately, there was talk of a young fellow down in the Panhandle who was blazing his way to the top. Still — if the hoodoo stayed on a vacation, and luck was with him — he might produce a champion this year.

Ranse had no doubt of it. Everything was coming his way — even Rita. Frequently he talked to her of marriage, and how he'd use the prize money he'd win at Coulée City for a brief honeymoon at Yellowstone Park, and she didn't say no. His love for her was his redeeming trait. It was the one big thing in his life.

One twilight, as they strolled home through the flowering field, it burst from him in a flood. "No man ever loved you like I do!" he cried hoarsely, his strained face bending close.

There was a responsive glow in Rita's eyes, but she held

off. "No-o?" she tantalizingly drawled.

Instantly the old, mad jealousy consumed him. "You think the hillbilly did? You call *him* a man? That white-faced, moonin' kid. Bah!"

It wasn't the insult to Montana that made Rita's cheeks flame. But in detracting from one who admired her, Ranse seemed to detract from the object of that admiration, herself.

"He was man enough to ride Yellow Peril," she lashed out with a fury from which Ranse shrank.

They stared at each other with faces set and anger-heated, their minds leaping back to that suspenseful moment when Ranse had stood before Yellow Peril in the chute, coincident with Montana's coming.

"Like heck he rode him," Ranse raged.

Fatally the girl taunted: "He was man enough to try."

Business called Dan Hurn to the city the following day, and in his absence the hoodoo worked overtime. Again a bleeding, unconscious form was carried into the ranch house. Again a cowboy tore across the plains. Again the sickening scent of drugs drifted through the open window to the group outside, waiting for the doctor's verdict, waiting in fear and trembling to face Dan Hurn.

But when Hurn heard what the doctor had to say, he was too crushed to recriminate, even to care how it came about. This was the end. No man could buck a hoodoo.

"I'll quit." Fatalistically he accepted defeat. "It's got me this time. First Monty, then. . . . But ten years. . . . God!"

But hope dies hard. As weeks passed, Hurn's hope in its dying struggles seized upon one last, meager straw. It was too tenuous a straw even to support hope; and hope sank as the days clicked off; the rodeo would be in Coulée City in seven more.

This night Dan Hurn was sitting on the verandah, head bent, brooding, when the crunch of gravel made him lift his eyes. A patriarchal figure on a small mule was toiling up the drive. Suddenly all the blood in Hurn's body seemed throbbing in his throat.

"Jude," he cried thickly, "is Montana back?"

He was an age waiting for the answer, formulating his own answers. Yes, for Jude was here. No, for he did not smile.

"He's back." There was something sorely disquieting in Jude's seamed old face, and in his tone. "He wants you, Dan. Will you come?"

XII
" 'I RODE HIM, AN' I WASN'T SCARED!' "

So it came to pass that Dan Hurn stood with Jude in the heart of the hills and murmurous forests, in the little valley that was the dwelling place of peace; stood with Jude beside the log corral, looking at a kingly bay, who returned his look with proud, hostile eyes; looking with wonder at Montana, tattered, confident, eager-eyed, as when he first came to Big Horn Ranch, and bidding his racing heart "Whoa!" as he listened to the strange tale Montana told.

"He ain't yellow." The boy's shining eyes were on the bay. "He's the best horse you got. The heart went out of him down there, where there wasn't no hills, no trees, no freedom. But he's got his nerve back here. He's pure dynamite . . . like Jeff said."

"An' you rode him?" Although he had forsworn his dream in the presence of the last victim of the rodeo hoodoo, Dan Hurn was breathing like a runner.

"I rode him till he mired in the swamp, an' couldn't move. I've rode every mustang here. Something went out of me, too, down there, but the hills give it back. I've got my ol' grip again, but" — there was more than a hint of pride in Montana's eyes — "I won't talk about me. I want you should see."

Under their gaze, he snubbed and saddled the stallion who proved he had lost none of his fiery spirit in that fray which ended in a draw and the valley swamp. Hurn, watching his swift, sure handling of the horse, felt that it was the old Montana. The doctor had said it would take time for his nerves to get over the shock. He'd had time and peace and quiet. Hurn noted that the bay shuddered with suppressed fury as Montana mounted, smiling and cool-eyed, and still he was reluctant to hope. The boy might be a flash rider, and. . . .

It was the last doubt Dan Hurn had, for that instant the snub rope whipped back, his self-control was knocked galley-west, as boy and horse skyrocketed into a repetition of that battle they had fought all over the vale.

Jude, who could not bear to see Montana in the saddle since that fatal day at Big Horn, wandered off alone. He was too old, he guessed, for so much strife. He'd go down to the cabin and sit a spell, out of the sun. Bending his feeble steps down the valley, he thought of the night Montana had come home — had stumbled into the cabin on Angel's Peak, an unrecognizable figure, all mud and blood and tatters, sobbing in a very delirium of joy: "Oh, Jude, I rode him . . . an' I wasn't scared." Even then he had seen it in the boy — this change.

"Seven days shalt thou wrestle with thy soul; seven nights shall evil haunt thee; and how thou shalt come

forth from that struggle, no man shall know."

Not seven days had Montana wrestled, but three times seven. And how had he come forth? Victor over fear — with God-given dominion? Yes, Jude knew that, could tell it by the fearful racket startling the birds from the thickets, rending the very vale, could tell it by the incoherent ravings of Dan Hurn.

Yet Montana was evil-haunted. His eyes could not bear the scrutiny of other eyes, but masked their secret well. What had changed him, aged, and hardened him? Was it love for the red-lipped girl down there? But love was ennobled. He could not possibly have heard what had happened at Big Horn Ranch. Was it jealousy of the light-haired rider? In human compassion Jude could no longer call him fool. Keen reader of thoughts that he was, Jude could not tell. He only knew that some fire was burning up the boy's better nature. Sitting there in the shade on the cabin steps, he prayed God to show him the fuel that fed it that he might reserve it before Montana went back to be hopelessly embittered when he learned that the girl he loved was. . . .

Suddenly he was conscious that the uproar had ceased. All was still — at peace. Jude sighed quietly. *How blessed peace was. Yet how men fight from it. Pretty soon he'd be on the other side of Jordan,* he thought, not regretfully. He wished he could see Montana settled first, and at peace. But this life with Hurn — this wasn't the way to peace.

Wearily leaning his white head back against the rough log wall, he saw them coming. The boy was reeling, as a deep-sea sailor reels in his first few steps ashore, and Hurn was putting a steadying arm around him. What a battle it must have been.

"You see, I ain't yellow," the boy's voice drifted singingly.

Hurn's sang, too, a richer, deeper note. "I'll tell the world you ain't. I never thought you was. My hat's off to you an' Dynamite both. I never saw a prettier rumpus."

"You'll take me back?" the boy's voice broke on the high note of his song.

"I'll say I will."

"I can ride at Coulée City?"

"You'll ride to Pendleton!"

"You think I'll stand as good a show as Ranse?"

Jude's heart leaped to his throat, and he bent tensely forward, dreading the answer. Hurn would tell him now. But no. . . .

"Yes, Monty" — surely the boy must notice the queerness of Hurn's tone — "you'll stand a better show than Ranse."

"Gee," Montana sighed, much too excited to note. "There's been times up here when I'd give the world with a ring around it to see the bunch. How's everybody? How's Ri. . . ."

"A right pretty spot . . . this valley."

Jude blessed Dan Hurn for that swift turn of subject. Could he hold the boy to it? Yes. For he had touched the one chord that could.

"Purty ain't all." Montana's enthusiasm struck a responsive spark in Jude. "See the grass on them slopes? Feed for a thousand cows. See all this river bottom? I'm puttin' it in timothy for winter feed. An' I'm goin' to build a road out. I got water grade all the way."

Hurn's stride broke, and he looked at the boy intently. "But you ain't a rancher, Monty . . . you're a rodeo man." For no comprehensible reason, Hurn thought of Sonny then.

"Yeah . . . I'm dreamin'," rejoined the boy.

Then they sat down on the steps with Jude, sociably silent, as men often are, when there is plenty of time and too much to say. Hurn was staying over tonight, and Montana would follow him down in a day or so.

"I've got to go back," the boy said suddenly, forgetting their presence and speaking his thoughts aloud. "I've got to go back to do two things."

"What you got to do, Monty?" Hurn's question was idle, but Jude leaned down to search Montana's eyes.

"Ride Yellow Peril, an'. . . ."

"Ride Peril?" Hurn's face went white under his healthy tan. "Not if I know it. The minute I go back, I'm goin' to have him shot. It's too much like abettin' murder to keep a beast like that."

The boy stared back, as pale, more resolute. "I've got to," he said fiercely. "I've got to ride him to show folks I ain't afraid. To prove to myself I ain't afraid. I've got to make sure I won't see him rearin' to strike at me again."

Hurn saw the point. But too recently he had seen the actual results of Peril's striking. "I won't allow it." Once and for all he'd settle that.

But the boy flashed back with taut defiance. "The next horse I ride will be Yellow Peril."

"But, Monty. . . ." A desperate gesture of impatience cut him short.

"I'm ridin' Peril next," vowed Montana, "or I don't ride."

Hurn realized he meant it. If Montana wouldn't ride again till he rode Yellow Peril, why — he must ride. And if he rode. . . . A staggering idea smote Dan Hurn, who was first and last a showman. "Care where you ride him, Monty?" Inspiration had brought him to his feet.

"No." Montana showed his wonder.

"Then," cried Hurn, and, as his idea unfolded, he paced rapidly before them, "we'll make it an exhibition ride! I'll put it on the bill at Coulée City. I'll advertise it all over the country. I'll light a fire under the whole state of Montana. Every he-man who hears of it will part with his last nickel to see Yellow Peril rode."

"I'll go right back with you." The boy was carried away with excitement, too.

"You'll stay right here," Hurn contradicted, his dramatic instinct in the ascendant. "You won't show up in this till you climb on that killer's back, the second day of the rodeo. A mysterious rider on Yellow Peril. See? Nothin' gets 'em like a mystery. You'll miss the regular contests, but I'll hold up the rodeo committee for a purse that will more than make up to you what you might make in prizes. Monty, if you ride Peril, your reputation's made."

Because every moment was precious, and there were suddenly a thousand things to do, Dan Hurn didn't wait for morning but started home at once. From Big Horn Ranch, in the morning, he would launch a campaign of advertising that would set a fire under Montana state, that would create the biggest sensation in rodeo history.

Montana stayed on in the valley with Jude to await the day of his spectacular début and great ordeal. To him the wait was long. But Jude found it all too short. What was this fire Montana nursed? If he were only the frank, open-hearted boy he'd been, he could talk to him, prepare him for what he must learn down there. But he stood in awe of him now, as of a stranger, and dared not ask. For once he had blundered and driven Montana from him.

Tonight, their last night here, they sat before the cabin, while the red fires of sunset shone through the boughs. Montana thought of all that had passed since that April day he'd ridden out of the hills with Jude. He'd gained the world, and lost it. Would he win it again? Or would he see the awful vision, and be thrown — to have those hoofs rear, real, no imagination then.

He'd know tomorrow. He'd be leaving here. Curiously he felt his going was traitorous to the girl he'd envisioned sharing his exile, that she did not approve. She'd be in the door, in the gingham dress that matched her eyes, watching, waiting. But she was a dream. He was done dreaming. At this time tomorrow he'd be with the bunch, with Calgary, Kid, and Rita. . . .

"Son" — at last, anxiety wrenched the word from Jude — "you told Dan Hurn you had *two* things to do."

The boy started. "Yeah . . . ride Peril."

"And the other, son?"

The pent-up flood burst its dam. It surged in all its force behind the eyes raised to Jude — eyes that were masked no longer.

"Pay Ranse back!" Montana winced at the way Jude shrank from him, with some unfathomable horror in his face, and, jerking the piece of cinch from his shirt, he burst out hotly: "It ain't account of Reet, but . . . Jude, see here! He cut this cinch the time I rode Peril. He tried to kill me. He was to blame for all the hell I've been through. An' if it's the last thing I ever do, I'm goin' to pay him back."

There was a long pause, filled by the soft music of wind-stirred leaves. Then, reverently, as of something that is done, and not to be, Jude quavered: " 'Vengeance is mine . . . I will repay, saith the Lord'."

With the sullen tinge that marked the change in him, the boy muttered: "I sure don't aim to trouble the Lord with Ranse."

XIII
" 'RIDE 'IM, COWBOY!' "

Crowds! Thrills! Stifle and din and dust! Bronze-faced 'punchers with spraddle legs. Sioux squaws in blankets and beads. Blackfoot bucks in feathers and deerskin. Cute papooses with shoe-button eyes. Wranglers, ropers, cowgirls, and everyday folks. Smell of horses, humanity, and barbecued meat. Creak of leather, jingle of spurs, cheers, jeers, and thunder of hoofs. Dizzy chaps, rainbow-ish shirts, filigreed boots and vests and hats. Rodeo!

The grandstand groaned under a double load of sweltering humans. Saddle horses fringed the infield fence the whole mile around. A fair share of the population of Montana, heeding Hurn's impassioned call, had massed in the Coulée City arena, ready to part with its last nickel to see Yellow Peril ridden, ready to borrow another nickel to bet it couldn't be done, to bet it was all a hoax, framed up by that wily purveyor, Dan Hurn, to get the crowd to bet on any old thing, as a highly excited rodeo gathering bets.

With three outfits like Hurn's whooping it up, and men and horses fresh, the roundup was going off with a bang, with Dan Hurn's riders covering themselves with glory, and Dan Hurn's name on every tongue.

Who was this mysterious *hombre* with the suicidal intention of tackling the killer? Where was his keeper? Why was he running at large? Rodeo followers from all over the West turned their backs on the show to debate that, or throng about the pen next to the chute where the man-killer, Yellow Peril, held court.

Individually and *en masse*, they besieged Hurn's outfit to no avail. Not one of them knew. Hurn wouldn't tell. He just grinned at them — a maddening, small-boy grin — and bade them wait and see. Well, there wasn't much longer to wait, for the ride would take place the second day of the rodeo.

This was the second day.

"It's a cinch it's none of us," Kid assured Calgary, when they found themselves side-by-side in the jam, right after the bulldogging, and with time to mop their faces and breathe. "Ranse was the only one of us who had a chance with Peril, an' it sure ain't Ranse."

"Nope," Calgary agreed, and there was a vestige of animosity in his face as he referred to him now, "it sure ain't Ranse."

"Well, we'll know *pronto*," Kid said thankfully, "for they're announcin' the relay race . . . an' Peril's next."

The time nearing for which everyone had waited two long days of suspense, the throng thickened about the killer's pen.

"None of him in my dish," affirmed a long-coupled wrangler from Powder River, as Yellow Peril returned their stare with wicked eyes and bare, heavy teeth. "Five notches is a heap too many for a hoss."

"Then you heard about the last one?" queried a grimy bronc' buster, hailing from Cheyenne.

Powder River said: "Yeah . . . pretty tough."

Soberly they turned back to the track as a prodigious cheer went up. The relay race was on. The horses thundered once around the track and back. A vividly pretty girl in red was in the lead. Jumping from her horse before it stopped, she jerked off the saddle and, running to the fresh horse waiting, slapped it on, gave one jerk to the cinch, made a flying mount, and was off.

"Classy, li'le kid," Cheyenne admired, as she tore down the track on the second lap.

"Yeah," dittoed Powder River. "But Reet ain't so sparkly as she used to was. She's apt to find it pretty hard sleddin' now. Fer it's one thing to ride fer the sport of it, an' other because you have to."

"Game of her, though." Meditatively Cheyenne spat between the rails. "Jist goes to show you can't tell a hootenanny about women. They'll prance through life like life was a joke, till all of a sudden something jolts 'em hard, an'. . . ."

Thunderous cheers for the girl in red. While they were in progress, Hurn's men forced Yellow Peril into the chute.

Again Kid and Calgary found themselves together, as the man with the megaphone stood up in the judge's box, and a hush settled over them and the crowd.

"Nex' event, ladies and gentlemen," sonorously rolled the long-awaited announcement over the tense arena, "is an exhibition ride of the famous Hurn outlaw, Yellow Peril. . . ."

Cheers!

". . . the worst horse in the West! His trail has been a trail of blood an' sudden death. We won't recount his victims here. To many of you, they were friends. A purse of five hundred dollars donated by the show committee, with private donations totaling almost one thousand dollars, will be awarded the brave rider who hopes today to settle all scores. His name . . . but first we warn everybody to stay off the track. This is a finish ride, an' the horse is dangerous. . . ."

"Aw, Cripes, tell us something we don't know, you long-winded yahoo!" Impatiently Calgary apostrophized the man with the megaphone.

"So we repeat our warnin' . . . stay . . . off . . . the . . . track! Now, ladies, an' gentlemen, the name of this young rider, unknown to rodeo fame, is. . . ."

Just then Calgary's eyes sighted Dan Hurn's Stetson in the sea of hats, and all but leaped from their sockets. For Hurn was coming from under the grandstand, and with him — dolled up like a Christmas tree, in a sky-blue silk shirt and silver-trimmed chaps — was a young, slim somebody, who looked like, walked like, was. . . . Seizing Kid's arm in a grip that would leave a blue mark for many a day, Calgary shrieked: "Montana!"

Like two lunatics, they fought toward him through the cheering crowd. Men choked their way — stalwart 'punchers, who had held their place on that fence for hours, and had no intention of being dislodged now that the crucial moment had come.

"Lemme through!" shrieked Calgary, clawing at one of the stalwart backs. "Lemme through! He's my pal!"

Others of Hurn's riders had spotted Montana, too. They reached him at the same time, mobbed him, carried him bodily to the chute.

There was no time now to go into the mystery of how Montana came to be here — in all the contradiction to the last time they had seen him — ready to ride Yellow Peril, and the hero of the hour. No time even to think of it, now — for the crowd was waiting, Peril was waiting, saddled, and they all had their own part to play. So they wrung his hand, wished him luck, and left him there. There upon the fence, over the horse who had all but killed him and haunted him so long. But Montana didn't look at Yellow Peril. He stood up there, unconscious that he was the cynosure of some ten thousand eyes, sweeping the rodeo crowd — his first, as a performer — for sight of the girl he loved, whom he still called Rita. He hated the crowd for hiding her. Would she root for him? Would she remember that other ride, when he had worn her colors, and trailed them in the dust?

He ceased to look, and, as the throng twisted and turned for a glimpse of him, swung his leg over the yellow killer.

"Nervy cuss, anyhow," affirmed Powder River.

"Nervy! Holy Smoke!" cried Cheyenne, who had only that moment learned it himself. "That's the hillbilly Peril smashed up last spring."

A whisper of that ran through the crowd, intensifying their interest in this cool, dark rider who had come out of the hills to do a thing from which the hardiest of them quailed. It gave a personal note to the coming bout. Then a silence fell upon them. It was a mystery how five thousand people could be so still.

In the second's space, while he sat there in the saddle, Montana saw Kid and Calgary posted on opposite sides of the track, with loops made, and, across the track, a mounted man with drawn gun. He smiled at these precautions. He wouldn't need them. He didn't have the fear of a horse now — and Yellow Peril was just a horse.

Then, as the grandstand rose in a body, everybody mad to see and getting in everybody else's way of seeing, the tender swung the gate, falling over himself to get out of the road, and Yellow Peril, the very personification of equine wickedness, plunged onto the track.

Now! If ever a scene beggared description, that scene did.

"It was hell," is the best those who witnessed it can accomplish when quizzed. "Jist plain hell an' repeat!"

From the first frightful stiff-legged buck that throttled the cheers and left the spectators tense until it was over, Yellow Peril fought without quarter or mercy, by fair means and foul. His screams as he fought struck terror to every heart — the inarticulate, horrible voice of a berserk brute. With bawl on bawl, he writhed, pitched, snapping back and forth in stupendous, end-changing bucks, delivered with the force of thirteen hundred enraged pounds, that must surely be tearing the boy to pieces, knocking the very breath of life from his body. Yet he stuck. He couldn't stay for another spasm like that. He did! Easy, too — like he was riding any old horse. But one didn't get white like that on any old horse. It *was* tearing him to pieces. But he'd stick. He was that kind.

"Ya-ah, hang-g-g to 'im, kid!"

"Oh, you hillbilly!"

They held their breath, as the yellow fiend, crazed with the bloodlust, flashed up in a skyscraping twist, came down with a force that shook the grandstand, sunfished eight feet to the left, landed almost flat on his side, and was, with his intrepid rider, lost in the enveloping cloud of yellow dust. Surely the boy was a goner now. No man could have stayed on that.

Then they sighted his blue shirt through the dust, saw his spur flash high on the stiff, tawny neck, as Yellow Peril straightened in a series of backward, stiff-legged bucks enough to shake the boy's teeth from his head, and the whole five thousand onlookers went wild. Hats flew in the air. Men hugged each other. Women were hysterical.

"Ride 'im, Monty!" screamed Hurn's riders.

Down the track, between two solid lines of taut humanity, churning, leaping, screaming, fought the yellow killer, and Calgary, Kid, and the man with the gun kept pace.

It was a finish fight. Whose finish? The strength and fury and infernal cunning of all the powers of hell was in the lathered horse. One second they saw him rear back, back, as if to topple over and crush the rider, and, when the boy's spur raked his flank, bringing him down, he lurched into those mighty side-winding bucks that no rider had ever weathered before. Failing to unseat him, with nose to stifle joint, he put himself in motion like a spring-set top, and spun, and spun, until the watchers were dizzy and couldn't look.

Only the bravest of them could look now. For there was agony in the boy's face, a strained, set look that would haunt them for many a day, that grayed their own in sympathy. Agony and blood.

Then, in utter horror, they saw the frenzied devil slam himself against the fence, and slam, and slam. The boy's motions, as he swung his leg high to evade those blows, were heartbreakingly slow. No wonder. He wasn't made of iron. Oh, how the crowd hated that horse. How they wanted to see him ridden to a finish.

"Stick to 'im!" raved cowboys who had seen everything there was to be seen in the way of outlaw horses, and seen nothing that had prepared them for this. "H-h-hook 'im, kid!"

Calgary, twisting, turning with the battle, with rope ever ready, screamed, too, as tears cut down his dusty face: "He's my pal. Oh, Gawd . . . he's my pal!"

Did Rita see? Could this be Rita who sat with face in hands, unable to see it — this thrill of thrills.

Was this Dan Hurn, who hated himself, cursed himself, and wondered who he was that a man should go through that for him?

Was this Sonny, who stood with Jude and watched, dry-eyed?

Then the horse, landing with another pitching leap, doubled to his knees. . . .

"By might, he's got him!" yelled Dan Hurn.

It seemed so. For the yellow killer's jumps were slower, fewer, and he wasted no more energy in screams. By seconds his fury waned. At last, reeking from every pore, he stumbled against the inner fence. With barely life to see his chance, to know the battle over, Montana seized the rail and drew himself from the saddle, and Yellow Peril staggered a few steps down the track and stopped, a menace no longer, no longer a challenge — a broken, beaten, harmless horse.

The boy, leaning dazedly against the fence, with his blood roaring in his ears, heard the mad howling of the crowd above the roar, saw the sea of people sweeping toward him.

This was what he'd dreamed of — when he dreamed of being a rodeo rider for Hurn. Why? he wondered dully. What was it all about? What came of it? Dust! You went from one town to another — kicking up dust. That wasn't what dust was for. Dust was ground — to grow things in — trees — flowers — timothy. . . .

Calgary caught him as he swayed.

It was all a vague and incoherent dream to Montana — that he was lying on a cot in a hospital tent — that he'd ridden Yellow Peril — that he'd seen Calgary and the bunch, and they'd just cleared out to give him air and a chance to rest. So he wasn't much surprised when the person entering now turned out to be the girl he'd dreamed.

"I . . . I thought you'd be in gingham," he whispered.

She looked down at her shirt, blue like his, at her short, fringed leather skirt, and up at him, wide-eyed.

"Riding? In gingham?"

"Not ridin' . . . sewin', puttin' woman's fixin's on our

cabin, waitin' for me up there."

Almost as pale as he, she dropped down at his side, and he took her hand. "You was with me," he whispered, looking for the halo around her head, which wasn't there, for there wasn't any sun in the tent to make it. "I couldn't have stood it, if it hadn't been for you."

The girl whispered, searching his eyes, and with her very soul in hers: "Are you sure it was me?"

"Dead sure. I thought for a while it was someone else, but . . . I had dust in my eyes . . . rodeo dust. But I been up where folks see clear. I know now it's been you ever since kid days, when your hair was red, an' you slapped me for sayin' so. An' I found the ranch for us . . . you an' me . . . an' I got a thousand dollars to stock it with, so. . . ."

"I couldn't risk it" — there wasn't much jealousy in Sonny Hurn, but just enough to pique her to that speech — "I couldn't risk your having another spell when you couldn't see me for . . . dust." Then she couldn't bear to see him so miserable after all he'd been through, and said softly: "Tell me about our ranch."

But he didn't know that was capitulation. With the keener appreciation one feels for a loved thing lost, he told her about the little valley where he'd found himself, and gone down into the tules with Dynamite, of the cabin he'd planned for her on the rise, right handy to the spring, of the land he'd clear and fence, and the swamp he'd drain. . . .

"No," she put her little boot smack down on that, "we won't drain the swamp."

All at once Montana was sitting up on that cot as if Yellow Peril had never been, his dark face aglow with rapture, a thousand joy bells ringing in his soul.

"You'll come?" he breathed, looking deep into her eyes.

"I'll come."

"You'll give up all this" — with a gesture toward the roar and babble of tongues that pulsed to them — "to go up there alone with me and live?"

"To live," said Sonny Hurn.

As they reached this highly satisfying conclusion, Dan Hurn, who had approached the tent with the laudable intention of felicitating Montana, and been shocked by the text of the words drifting out into remaining to eavesdrop, walked heavily off, his face a strange study in mixed emotions.

The hoodoo had struck again.

XIV
" 'YOU'RE FIRED!' "

Everything was so wonderfully right with Montana, loving Sonny, knowing Sonny loved him, and with money to make every dream come true, that it was long before he realized that something was radically wrong with the rest — not, in fact, until after he was entirely over the effects of his ride, and milling about with the crowd, having a regular reunion with his old friends. Even then he couldn't lay a finger on just what was wrong.

They'd be talking along about old times, then, all of a sudden, look down in the mouth, and switch the subject. He'd noticed the same thing in Jude and Dan Hurn. It struck him as queer that he'd seen neither Rita nor Ranse. Naturally Ranse wouldn't go out of his way to hunt him up, but, as Hurn's star rider, he ought to be the most conspicuous man on the track. Yet he wasn't here. It dawned on Montana that it was from any mention of Rita or Ranse that the bunch shied off.

"Where's Ranse hidin' out?" He experimented on Calgary first.

Sure enough, Calgary looked glum, swallowed hard, and said vaguely: "Oh, around. Criminy, pal, you should 'a' seen the Panhandle Kid on. . . ."

Passing up Calgary, he tried it on Kid: "Where's Reet?"

Again that sorry look, gulp, and evasion. "Reet? Oh, yeah, Monty, there's a Palouser down here I want you to meet."

So it continued, and Montana was worried. He hated a mystery — it made you think. He didn't want to think of a thing but Sonny and the ranch they'd make out of the valley with this money he'd won.

Worming his way through the press, he kept a close look-out for the pair on whom his friends were so mysteriously mum. Thinking of Ranse, looking for Ranse, he remembered that one of the things he'd vowed to do up in the hills was still to be done. He'd been worlds too happy even to. . . .

Someone reached out of the crowd, catching his arm.

"Monty, I want to congratulate you on that ride!"

It was Rita. Rita, whose hair was midnight in the star shine, but whose red lips did not laugh, might never have laughed. That was the first difference Montana marked, the total, pitiful absence of laughter in Rita Sills.

"Where you kept yourself, Reet?" He was genuinely glad to see her, but wondered how he could ever have thought that the feeling he had for her was love.

"We have to keep pretty well out of the crowd," she said simply, as if that would explain.

"We?"

"Why, Ranse and I." Then, seeing he still was at sea, she said, as if fearing that what she would say might cause him pain: "Surely you now, Monty, that I'm married to Ranse."

So this was what they were keeping from him. Rita was married. They thought he'd care.

"I didn't know." He smiled, as he held out his hand. "But I, wish you luck."

"Luck?" Oh, the pathos of that — of the wan little ghost of Rita's gay smile that showed through her tears as she took his hand. "Well, I sure need it. For, Monty, I've played out of luck from the start. I didn't know how much I loved Ranse until he was hurt, and. . . ."

Montana cried: "Hurt?"

"Why, haven't they told you? He was hurt on Yellow Peril three weeks ago. Oh, Monty, it was all my fault. I said things to Ranse that made him ride. He rode, and I . . . saw it." She put her hands up to her eyes as if to shut out something too awful, and the slim, red-clad shoulders shook.

Seeing that she was nearing a breakdown, Montana drew her out of the mob.

"It's just about killing me . . . to see him suffer," she cried, her dusky eyes dreadful with pain. "He would come today. He made us bring him . . . to torture himself by watching the rest of us . . . knowing he'll never be in it again."

There was a mighty lump in Montana's throat, and in his heart a bigger wonder that this — this sad-faced woman — was Rita — who couldn't stand sick folks, who laughed when a. . . .

"You mean he's hurt so he can't ride . . . ever?"

"Never," she told him. "Unless. . . ."

"Unless what, Reet?" he pressed, as she faltered.

"Unless a miracle happens," was her bitter comment. "Unless I win about every event this year. Figure his chance for yourself. For, Monty, he's. . . ."

Just then the people about them made way with all deference for something to pass, and Montana saw Ranse. He
was in a wheelchair — lying back, queerly — and the lower
part of his body seemed dead. But his eyes — as bold and
blue as ever — meeting Montana's, were startlingly alive.
But not with the old contempt — with envy, jealousy? —
yes, of two strong legs, of manhood.

Now, as Jude propelled the chair to Montana's side —
for, characteristically, the good Samaritan of Painted Buttes
had sought the most afflicted in all that throng to minister
to, and in his ministerings forgot personal wrong — Ranse
said slowly: "Once," and the strange quality of his gaze held
Montana's eyes, "I won money bettin' you wouldn't ride
Peril. Today, I bet it again an' lost. So, if you ever felt you
owed me anything, kid" — and Montana knew he referred
to the broken cinch — "it's paid. If Peril had got you, I
might have ridden again. Now I'm worse than dead . . .
crippled like this, out of all this, knowin' my wife has to ride
for two, knowin' I'm dependin' on. . . ."

"Don't, Ranse," Rita pleaded, bending to straighten his
pillow, and hide her eyes. When she raised up, Montana
saw that the last hint of a tear was gone; she was suddenly
brave, suddenly strong. Explaining that she was in the next
event and wanted Ranse to see her ride, she took the chair
from Jude, and slowly wheeled it away.

There were tears in Montana's eyes, too, as they fol-
lowed — tears washing away the last thought of revenge.
Vengeance belonged to God, Jude had said. God had used
Yellow Peril as the instrument of His vengeance. No — for
God wouldn't do that. But fate had done it, and he wished
fate hadn't. It was awful to see a big, husky fellow like
Ranse. . . .

"Some will say it was pity," murmured old Jude, his

grieved eyes on the pair, "an' some will say it's remorse for her blame. But, Monty, it wasn't. It was love made her marry him . . . the love of woman that passeth all understandin', that wants to cherish an' care for the one she loves. God help her carry her load."

"Ain't Ranse a chance?" Montana asked huskily.

Jude said: "In a way. You see, his spine's hurt. There's pressure somewhere . . . I don't just understand it. Rita says there's a doctor back East who can cure Ranse. But it costs so much . . . 'most a thousand dollars, she says . . . to get him back there an' all. Son, he was so sure no man could ride Peril that he bet every cent he could muster . . . an' lost. If he'd won, he'd have had enough to be cured."

Flashingly it came to the hill boy then what Ranse meant, when he said he might have ridden again if Peril had "got" him today. He knew now what Rita meant by a miracle, and said soberly: "Reet'll never be able to save that up."

They were silent together. All about them people were making a big hullabaloo, but they didn't hear.

"I . . . I reckon I'll sell off part of my flock," Jude was thinking out loud. "It's too big for me to look out for . . . alone."

Montana walked off. He knew what Jude meant by that sudden decision. Jude was pure gold. But he'd better hang onto what little he had. It couldn't help Rita and Ranse. Suppose it was he — just married, and crippled like that, and Sonny who had to do the riding for two.

A cloud had come over his day, and he went to hunt Sonny, and make more plans, so he could forget about Ranse. Things had sure switched since the day Ranse had made fun of his hat, since the day Ranse had him down. Now Ranse was down, and it would take a whole thousand dollars to get him up. And he, Montana, had a thousand dollars. His hand went to his shirt pocket in which the enveloped bills were carefully pinned. He had a thousand to buy cattle with and set up housekeeping.

Then he found Sonny, and the world was bright, and everything was wonderfully right. Together, after an hour or so, they went to take Sonny's father and mother into their plans.

They found them in the cook tent of Hurn's Wild West Show, deep in a confidential discussion with Jude. And not altogether unprepared, it would seem, to see them enter like this — very self-conscious, hand in hand — for all three looked exceedingly wise.

"Well, speak up!" boomed Dan Hurn with paternal severity. "What's your prospects, young man?"

"That's what I wonder." Montana grinned. "We hit Lewiston next, don't we? Well, I'm goin' in for first prize in the buckin' horse contest. What do you think of my chance?"

To say Dan Hurn was dumbfounded is putting it mildly. "Why . . . I . . . ," he sputtered, "I thought you was a rancher . . . not a rodeo man."

Sonny wasn't a white anemone now, but a pink, pink rose.

"You listened, Dad?" she accused him, from Ma Hurn's embrace.

"An' I got an earful," he shamelessly said. "What I heard somehow conveyed the impression that you was both goin' in for the simple life. Then what's this about goin' on with the show?"

"It takes money to live . . . even up there." The boy was dead serious. "An' I need the money, so. . . ."

"Waal," commented Hurn, with a broad wink at Jude,

"it won't take a fortune to keep Sonny in her accustomed style. A thousand ought to make a fair start."

"I ain't got a thousand," Montana said desperately. "I ain't got a cent."

Again Hurn couldn't credit his ears. "If you ain't, you're some spender. Where's that money you just won on Peril?"

Montana, embarrassed, silently twisted his hat, and Jude came to his rescue. "He give it to me, Dan," the old man said proudly, "to give to Ranse."

"Waal, I'll be. . . . After the way he done you dirt from first to last. After the thing he. . . . Is this some of Jude's teachin's? Heapin' coals of fire on Ranse's head? Overcomin' evil with good? Doin' to others as you would. . . ."

"It ain't nothin' like that," earnestly said Montana. "Ranse ain't ever to know where it come from. But I" — he couldn't express it — "I want to be happy myself, an' I can't be happy while he ain't got a chance. Sonny felt jist like me. You see, we can ride. An' so, we'll work this season. . . ."

"Not for me!" Hurn exploded. "You're fired!" He chuckled loudly at their utterly dumbfounded look.

"I mean it," he said. "Here, I was gittin' the kick of my life out of bein' a martyr, an' you spoil it all. It's no go, son. Ma an' Jude, here, an' me, had this all settled an' sealed. We'll see you through. I got more cows at Big Horn than I can handle, and I'll give you. . . . Hold on, don't get on your high hoss," — as he read protest in Montana's eyes. "I didn't mean give. But I been lookin' for a likely young fellow to take my beef stock on shares. You seem to have the qualifications, an' what's more . . . the range. But we'll go into that later. What do you think about that, honey?"

"I don't know whether to be mad or glad," Sonny owned

106

candidly. "We thought you'd raise the roof about losing Montana, and here you won't take him as a gift. What's wrong with you, Dad? What about the star for your crown?"

Hurn's smile faded. "What's wrong with me?" he soberly echoed. "Danged if I know. Old age, mebbe. I can't take the breaks like I used to, for these last few jolts have hit me hard. I know Monty *could* be champion, but, as a son-in-law, I prefer him a rancher . . . they're twicet as durable. So I'll manage to run the show with the rest of the boys, an' you two fix up to go homesteadin'. That's how Ma an' me got our start . . . on the Big Horn, thirty years ago. We hadn't nothin' but a ramshackle buckboard, an old muley cow, an' a cayuse team, did we, Ma?" He sentimentally patted Ma's hand. "Now, what do you say, Jude?"

Thus appealed to, Jude gazed long at the young folks, who loved him, and who he loved so well, then, through the open side of the tent, his old eyes sought the far, blue-misted hills to which he was not returning alone, and out of the fullness of his heart, he quavered: "God is good."

The Throwback

I
"A THROWBACK"

Someone had told Jess Trailor that he could not live honestly on Big Smoky range. Here, where his father Ute Trailor, had lived and died by violence — a rustler; where his brother Dan had followed in his father's crooked footsteps to the tragic last. For back of the community's hate for the Trailors were years of crime, and the memory of a good man slain.

But Jess, last of his name, had been undaunted. He would live down the past, of which he had never been a part, and make his name as good as any man's, now that no one was responsible for it but himself. So, a year ago, he had vowed, and now. . . .

To go back. In the beginning, and on a day no man marked, Ute Trailor, with his two infant sons, had drifted into Big Smoky range. High in a wild and lonely cañon, that ran like a blue vein in the stern face of the loftiest mountain in that lofty mountain chain, he established headquarters. While his boys grew up — in an environment as favorable for physical growth as it was for bringing out the worst that is in even the best of men — Ute pursued his lawless calling. He lived, like the buffalo wolf, on the fat rangelands below, and, like the wolf, outwitted pursuit in the wilds above.

Many times in the years of his wolfish sojourn here, Ute had taken to the hills. But that September day one year ago, he had started just a fatal shade too late. The posse of angry ranchers, determined to halt the depredations of the rustling Trailors, had overtaken and eternally stopped old Ute.

Three weeks later, Dan — then just turning twenty-one — had been surprised and killed in a cattle raid. Dan, in dying, had greatly enhanced the black luster of the family name by taking a popular young deputy with him "over the range."

Thus the boy, Jess, had been left alone in the little blue cañon, with nothing but the old log cabin and corrals, bitter memories, and the unbeatable handicap of a hated name. That it was unbeatable, Jess had not known last September, and he had resolved above all else to keep his feet on the highroad of life.

This he confided to Ford Cruze, an old pal of his father's, who rode down often to see how "Ute's boy" was getting on and to insist on Jess's coming to live with him. A plea that the boy had to refuse, since he knew — although Big Smoke did not — that Ford Cruze was a rustler. Neither could he avoid Ford, as he did the other men who had hung about the cabin in Ute's time, for the genial old rascal was the only friend he had on earth. It was Ford who told him that it was impossible for a Trailor to live honestly on Big Smoky range.

Now, a year later, it was a mystery to Ford how Jess had lived. Honestly, he knew, for in all his twenty years of life the boy had been as straight as the proverbial string.

But to the range at large it was no mystery. When a man lived with no visible means of support, it meant but one thing to cowmen, when rustlers were abroad, and meant it beyond all shadow of doubt when that man was the dead Trailors' kin'.

Only Jess knew how terribly hard that year had been. Often he lived on straight venison for weeks — the lucky weeks. Hunger lost all novelty for him. He hunted his living, when he was not hunting work — and with more success. Although he persistently hunted work on every ranch that hired men, there was not room on Big Smoky's payroll for a Trailor. Jess had not drawn a day's wages in that year.

Now and then, however, he went down to Salitas with a few coyote ears or cougar scalps, on which he collected the state bounty, and so bought the supplies or clothing of which he stood in greatest need.

But the strain of this existence, the constant temptation, unmerited suspicion and ostracism, loneliness and shame, might well have broken the strongest spirit. And Jess, facing winter penniless, was dangerously near agreeing with Ford Cruze, when the tide seemed to turn.

The Salitas Stampede, for which that range lived from year to year, announced its gate-crashing event — a bucking horse contest, in which Big Smoky cowboys would ride for the local championship and a purse of five hundred dollars in gold. Then, for the first time, Jess dared hope. If he won, he would have not only a winter stake and a start in the spring, but some small claim on the community's respect.

Tomorrow was the last day of the Stampede.

Today, out in the corral in the cottonwoods, Jess prepared for his ride. Entirely surrounded by twine, rivets, and lace leather, he was putting repairs on his saddle, when a booming voice from behind startled him: "Howdy, son! Cobblin' up ol' three-in-one?"

Jess swung to see a blaze-faced black in the trail. Its rider's amused gaze was bent on the old jigsaw puzzle of pieces and patches that passed for a saddle.

"Yeah, Ford." Jess grinned. "It'll be brand-new, when I get done."

Ford Cruze chuckled. He looked like anything but a rustler, leaning ahead in the saddle, watching Jess. A big man, easy in manner and movement, with genial eyes, a kind, lined, old cinnamon face, and hair that showed touches of frost under his black sombrero.

"Waal," he said, with a twinkle, "you can't disguise that ol' shell but what I'll know it. One of them stirrups was Dan's. T'other was Ute's. The tree's about all that's left of your ol' original. When you goin' to pension it an' get a regular one?"

Quietly, taking his breath away, Jess said: "Tomorrow . . . if I'm lucky, Ford."

Over the old rustler's face broke a startled gleam. "How come? Some *hombre* turned human an' give you a job?" he cried.

The boy denied that, and went on wrapping a strip of soaked rawhide about the naked steel of the saddle horn.

"What then?" Ford pressed.

The boy turned and, leaning back against the fence, looked fully into the eyes of his friend. "I'm ridin' in the contest," he said.

Ford released a long-held breath. "Waal," he predicted with odd finality, "you won't be lucky."

"Why not?" Jess flashed, for, without vanity and barring accident, he knew he stood every chance. "I ain't such a slouch of a rider as all that."

"No," — and in Ford's slow admission there was singular, almost personal pride — "you can ride, Jess. I'd say you could ride rings around any man in Big Smoky. You ought to . . . it's all you ever done. While the other boys who'll ride tomorrow were growin' up with games an' such,

111

you was up here in the hills ridin' wild ones for fun. Why, I mind" — and his eyes smiled down — "gettin' the scare of my life once, when I run across you up on Baldy a-straddle of a wild mustang that you'd roped yourself. You . . . just a spindle-shanks, Jess, an' bareback to boot. An' him runnin' wild through the trees, fightin' loco. I thought you was a gone coonskin for sure, but you rode him to a standstill."

"Then," insisted Jess, "why won't I be lucky tomorrow, Ford?"

The man hesitated. Jess waited, dread in his dark, eager, sensitive face, his slim body tense. As he was then, against the silvery trunks of the cottonwoods, Ford never forgot him. At that moment he felt more deeply than ever that something different, compelling, about Jess Trailor, a suggestion of unusual strength to be unleashed for good or evil, as the course of his life would run: strength, not of body alone, but of spirit.

This spirit looked out of his eyes. They were of a peculiar, burning blue, under straight, black brows, the eyes of a fighter. Slightly and attractively oblique, they were the one feature Jess had shared with Dan and inherited from Ute, the one feature noted by Big Smoky range — Trailor eyes.

"What I meant, Jess," said Ford, and those eyes burned on him as he spoke, "is . . . you'll lose, if you win. This range ain't apt to give the decision to a Trailor."

"They can't help it!" fiercely declared the boy. "They've got to play fair. If I put up the best ride. . . ."

"They can't be fair," soberly Ford struck in. "They're only human, Jess. An' human nature's a mighty inhuman thing. Allow as how the judges want to act fair an square, an' suppose, for example, that Met Fergus is ridin'. Will they just see Met's performance? Or will they be seein', too,

the Seven Star Ranch, the obligations they owe his dad, an'
Jim Fergus hisself in the grandstand? It'll work like that for
every favorite son. An' it'll work the opposite for you, who
ain't a favorite son . . . by no means, but the son of the despised Ute Trailor."

The boy cried — "I don't care!" — his tremor pro-
claiming how much he cared. "I ain't askin' no favors. All I
want is a square deal."

"All you'll get," Ford said coldly, because it was the cold
truth, "is a raw deal. Jess, Jim Fergus won't be in the grandstand tomorrow . . . like we was supposin'. He's slated for
the king row."

Jess flinched as from a physical blow. Jim Fergus was
one of the judges tomorrow. To judge him — a Trailor!

"But," he faltered gamely, "he's the only one."

"He's the one," Ford reminded him grimly. "As Fergus
goes, so goes Big Smoky range."

Because it was the truth, and none knew it better than
Jess, there was despair in his heart as he turned back to the
saddle and mechanically fumbled the rawhide strips.

"Son," — full of sympathy, Ford got down and went up
to him — "I feel sort o' responsible for you since Ute
cashed in. 'Most like you was my own. It sure hurts to see
you wearin' yourself out on a losin' fight. Boy, throw in
with me. Collect a few of the wages of sin. . . ."

"Like Dad did . . . an' Dan?" broke in the boy, tight-
lipped.

"Like me, Bart, Seminole, an' the rest." Ford passed a
long arm about Jess. "Son, what's wrong with you? I don't
savvy you a bit. Neither did Ute, an' you worried him a
heap. Dan was a chip off the ol' block, but you . . . a throwback, Ute always said. A queer chick for a Trailor to hatch.
Where did you get these holy notions, Jess?"

113

"I . . . don't . . . know," the boy said slowly. Nor did he, yet.

Ford's arm tightened in sheer affection. "Son, I've watched you this last year. Believe it or not, I hoped you'd make the grade. But you can't . . . not here, you can't . . . with folks r'arin' to push you back two steps for every one you gain. You're just layin' up grief for yourself tomorrow, but," said the old man persuasively, as restlessly Jess stirred, "if you're dead set on it, let me help. At least, let me buy you a saddle that will stand the gaff."

"No!" the boy cried sharply, tempted almost beyond restraint.

Hurt by that refusal, Ford's arm dropped. "Tainted money, huh?" he suggested.

"That ain't why," earnestly protested Jess. "I'd take it like a shot, if I could pay you back. But I can't, unless . . . Ford, don't get me wrong. I ain't no plaster saint. I . . . I don't know what I am. But I'm tryin' hard to win out this way, because I seen enough to know the other way don't pay."

"Has this way paid?" Ford's eyes swept Jess from shapeless hat to leather chaps, as patched and in need of patches as the ancient saddle on the fence, seeing — the boy felt — all his poverty and shame, even the hungry days, in that one glance.

"Has this way paid?" Again, mercilessly, Ford asked, and in very mercy answered himself. "You know it ain't. Why, folks ain't even got the respect for you they had for Ute. They had the respect of fear for him . . . an' that's something, Jess. They paint you black as him, whisper about you, an' gang up against you. Why can't you get a job? Good men are scarce here. An' you're good. You know the cattle game from A to Z. There's your answer. You know the cattle game, an' you're a Trailor. Oh, I've heard talk."

The boy had a desperate, hunted look, and Ford urged: "Come on, Jess . . . be yourself. You can't be guiltier than folks think you are. Get the game, as well as the name. Come on up to my place, an' let me put you in the way of easy money."

A shudder went through Jess Trailor from head to foot. "Not your way, Ford . . . not yet."

Ford said no more then. But when he was in the saddle again, with shortened rein and Blaze's head turned up the trail that climbed the ridges — now aglow with autumn's fiery hues — to the bluer heights of his own cañon, he lingered, loath to leave. For he knew all the torture in store for Jess on the morrow. Hot anger rose within him that such things could be, and, also, the wish to leave some word with Jess, something that would be with him then — let him know he was not alone.

"Son," he said huskily, "you're in a blind alley. Someday you'll see that. Tomorrow, or a year from tomorrow . . . no matter. When you get to the end, I'll be there."

His sincerity did what no persuasion, starvation, or heartache had done — wrung from the boy his fateful promise.

"Ford," Jess cried, sudden tears quenching the fire in his eyes, "I'm goin' to ride in the Stampede! But if they give me the deal you say they will, I'll give up. I'll go Trailor."

II
"MEMORIES"

Just as the sun went down behind the black peaks, Jess finished with the saddle. The thoughts Ford had set in motion still raced through his mind. Sitting down on the cabin steps — too discouraged to think of supper — Jess let them race. He sat on for hours, while twilight drew a violet veil over the cañon, and darkening night closed in.

Why was he different from the other Trailors? That was the question Jess asked his heart, had been asking since Ford Cruze put it straight up to him. Ford said it had worried his dad. Well — the boy's lips twisted oddly — it had hurt him, put a barrier between his folks and him, so he couldn't get near them, although he loved them, couldn't even be pals with Dan.

"Heaven knows I never meant it to be," tensely he told the dreaming dusk. "Heaven knows I never felt superior to them. Anything but that."

Then why hadn't he just drifted into their way of doing before he got big enough to see it didn't pay? Before his dad and Dan got killed? When they were coaxing him to ride with them? For the first time in his life, Jess wondered at that. And, on the eve of the battle that would decide his life, the truth burst on him in a blinding flash.

Memory tracked it down, followed the lonely corridors of his heart back, back to the time when it was the heart of a lad, and flung a vivid scene from boyhood on the screen of his mind. Time: Four o'clock. Place: The schoolhouse at Salitas. Big Smoky kids bursting out the door like stabled colts. Among them, Jess saw himself, a boy of twelve, and before him Chuck Saunders, the tow-headed tattler of the class, jumping up and down, and chanting:

I know something I won't tell —
Three little darkies in a peanut shell!

Across the years, Jess heard the instant clamor of the rest for what Chuck knew, and his telling them in that fiendish chant: "Jetta Fergus likes Jess Trailor! I saw her give him that big apple in her desk!"

Then they were all shrilling like young coyotes, as they circled him and Jetta: "Jetta likes Jess! Jetta likes Jess!"

Instantly Jetta's brother, Met, had the tattler down in the dusty road, was on him, thumping him like the bully he had been even then, panting between blows, "You take that back! Take it back, or I'll kill you, Chuck! My sister wouldn't wipe her feet on that rustlin' scum!"

Then, while he had stood there, paralyzed with shame that burned him now, remembering, Jetta cried with scorn that silenced all, that stayed her brother: "Shame on you, Met Fergus. He's as good as we are. He can't help it what his folks does." And, throwing back her head like the little queen she was, Jetta defied her world: "I don't care what anyone says . . . I do like Jess!"

Kid stuff? Yes. But it is in the plastic years that things strike deeply, when a word may make or mar a life. Clay molds best when it is fresh. Although the scene faded, Jess felt again the same warm glow he had felt in childhood, the same blind adoration, worship, and even reverence for Jetta Fergus.

He knew with a shock that had a kind of horror in it, that this was why. This was why he had held out against his own flesh and blood — set himself apart from them, as people had put him away from them. This was why he had held out against Ford Cruze, why he had gone hungry rather than live on "easy money." Because, long ago, a girl had had the courage to stand up for him, and the only way he could vindicate her was to live up to her faith in him. He'd done that for — a Fergus. Incredulously he whispered the words, then began to laugh — a bitter, most unhappy laugh.

For Jim Fergus, of the Seven Star, had done more to make it impossible for the boy to do what his daughter had inspired him to do than anyone — than everyone. Fergus was Big Smoky's cattle king. As such, he had suffered most from the steady rustling of the Trailor gang. And he was an uncle of Sid Hollis, the young deputy whom Dan had killed. Fergus had cause to hate the Trailors, but. . . .

Leaning forward, every nerve and muscle tense, Jess cried in a choking tone: "He ain't got no monopoly on that." With natural, instinctive hatred, as his Trailor eyes glowed, phosphorescent in the night, he added: "Jim Fergus was in the posse that killed Dad."

He crouched there in the dark as memory threw other, awful pictures before his eyes: of the posse returning triumphant from its kill — bringing his father, like a slain wolf, home. Of his wild gallop through storm and night to the lonely siding where they told him he would find Dan. Of finding his brother — dead, in the reeking gramma grass, and of sitting close to Dan until dawn came, that his slicker might shield the dead boy from the rain. Memories that roused every drop of Trailor blood in his veins.

Now, fate had left it to Fergus to decide what was to become of the last Trailor. He would be one of the three judges tomorrow. But if he said black was white, any other two men in the country would sprain their tongues agreeing with him. The boy's jaw set. All right! It was up to Fergus. He would do his best to win. If he did, he would be on the highroad. If not — well, he had to live.

"But if he makes me go Trailor," the boy solemnly

vowed, "I'll make him sorry to the last day of his life."

Hours after he went to bed, Jess lay awake. The suffering had burned out in his blood, and hope in the coming contest was restored, but he could not sleep for thinking of Jetta. She had sure been sweet to him. Always taking his part. Telling him they couldn't lick him, if he kept his head up, and he always had. Fergus had taken her out of school right after that, and sent her to a girls' school down in Spokane. She just came home for holidays and summers. He had hardly seen her since — just a far glimpse, now and then, in Salitas or on the road, with one or another of the Big Smoky boys. They were all crazy about her.

He had not spoken to her since. She had been so good to him, he could not shame her. She would be ashamed of it — now that she was grown, now that folks had pinned the rustler sign on him. He wondered if she would be there tomorrow and see him ride. She might — almost everyone came home for the Stampede. But she would not know the stakes he was riding for — know that but for her he would have gone Trailor long ago.

The blue cañon ran like a black river. Coyotes howled in sad, wild, quavering cadence from its lonely brinks. Resultant of his thoughts, or prophetic of the morrow, Jess Trailor dreamed of a courageous, black-eyed slip of a girl defying all her friends: "I do like Jess!"

III
" 'LET 'ER BUCK' "

A record crowd packed the Salitas Stampede Grounds. The arena was a tangle of color, and ropes, and hoofs, and dust. Throbbing tom-toms and blaring bands. Hiving, excited buckaroos in dizzy chaps; cowgirls in sunset scarves; blanketed buck, and beaded klooch, rancher, trapper, trader, and what not? All festive in rodeo togs, all keyed to the last notch. Hundreds of cow ponies — they lined the infield fence the whole mile around — snorting and stamping as they caught the contagion. Prisoned, bucking horses, peering with murderous eyes through their bars — waiting.

Preliminary to the big event for which the throng had crashed the gates, man and beast went down the track in cyclonic action. The grandstand rocked with cheers, and waddies hooted or yipped from the corral tops. For this was the time for which that range lived from year to year — when excitement and danger walked hand in hand, when thrills were thrills, and the voice of the megaphone was raised in the land.

Through this wild tumult Jess Trailor rode his line-backed buckskin, rode with his burning eyes straight ahead, in his faded old shirt and bandanna, his frayed leather chaps, and hat that was — just a hat. He crowded through the seething mass until he came to the entrants' stand. Here, he slid down and, laying his entrance fee on the counter, asked the clerk to sign him for the big contest scheduled to take place soon.

The clerk blinked in surprise, started to say something, but swallowed it and complied. Having seen his name enrolled for his fateful ride, Jess turned away, hearing behind him the clerk's answer to some protester: "Sure. I know he's Jess Trailor, but he's a Big Smoky product . . . you can't rule him out."

An anxious bystander asked: "Can he ride?"

"Search me . . . but they say he's handy with a rope," was the reply.

A titter broke out. But Jess gave no sign of hearing the

speech, which, in range parlance, plainly accused him of rustling cows. He only carried his head a bit higher as he rode off, stabbed in the back by curious eyes.

Finding room for Bucky, his pony, among others at the infield fence, just across from the grandstand, Jess settled at the rail to wait and watch alone. Alone in a crowd — the worst kind of loneliness. More alone in this gathering of home folks than any stranger. Big Smoky had a word and smile for the stranger — but no use on earth for a Trailor. Eyes he knew looked straight through him, or turned away with a betraying swiftness.

A frantic cry rose in his heart. *Oh, Lord, let me win. So folks will forget I'm a Trailor. So they'll think of me as a rider . . . not a rustler.*

To still his nerves, he made a game of searching each pretty sombreroed face that went past, telling himself he might see Jetta. That this girl was she — no, Jetta's eyes were twice as black and bright. That one — going by? No, she wasn't pretty enough by half. But how did he know Jetta was pretty? It wasn't likely he would recognize her. Not in eight years had he seen her plain. Eight years was a long time. She'd be changed.

He wistfully watched the merry groups of 'punchers on stilt-heeled boots, scuffling and joking their way down the track. Gee, it must be fun to pal up like that, be one of a bunch of regular fellows. He never had. But maybe he would be after today. If he won, they'd look on him differently, maybe.

Five hundred dollars wouldn't mean much to the others. But to him — what wouldn't it mean to him. He tried not to think — he was nervous enough — tried to concentrate on the bulldogging, steer and calf roping stunts being pulled off, to applause that crashed like thunderclaps. But he was in a high fever of suspense when the cowgirl's race was announced, with the big feature next.

"Ridin', Chuck?" a spectator yelled at a stalwart 'puncher hobbling past.

"Sure am." Chuck grinned — that name Chuck Saunders had been the tow-headed tattler of Jess's class. "We all are, I reckon . . . but Met. He's tendin' chute. You know his ol' man's a judge. Good alibi."

Most of those in hearing laughed. Met Fergus had far more fame as a bully than as a bronc'-buster on his home range. But Jess did not laugh. It meant grief when his turn came at the chute. Met never missed a chance to take a slam at him. He had taken many before, and since that time, when they were kids and Met had called him "scum." He would have to take it, as he always had. With Jim Fergus in the king row, he couldn't risk a run-in with his son.

"So here's where you're hidin' out." At last somebody spoke to Jess. At a moment when everyone else was intent on the track, where a score of cowgirls were jockeying for a start.

Strung, quivering, as any racer at the wire, Jess looked at the man who had spoken to him — a wizened, watery-eyed cowhand, who had a sneaking coyote look about him and walked with a limp. It was Spike Travis, who Jess did not like or trust. And he could not believe that Spike liked him any better, in spite of this overture — not when he carried right with him, as he would to his grave, a constant reminder of his old grudge against the Trailors. For that limp of Spike's was the result of a bullet from the gun of Ute Trailor. They used to "work" together, and they had had some trouble. But Spike had reformed — or, anyhow, wormed himself into the good graces of Jim Fergus, and for a year now he had been working out at the Seven Star.

"I ain't hidin'," coldly Jess told Jim Fergus's man. "I don't have to hide."

"No?" drawled Spike, with fine sarcasm. "Well, that's a fine feelin'."

Jess shot back: "You ought to know!"

But as Spike dissolved into the crowd — now straining to follow the pounding horses in their neck-and-neck race around the track — Jess stared at the spot where he had been, suddenly afraid, and for the first time. If he got a raw deal, he had promised to go Trailor. Just seeing snakes like Spike. . . .

His eyelids narrowed, and hate blazed through. For there, so close he could have reached out and touched him, passed Jim Fergus, the prosperous, vindictive old cattle king. He was going up to the judges' stand, going to decide if a Trailor could "live honest" on Big Smoky range, going to decide if the last Trailor would go straight, or, maybe, wind up like his father and brother.

Dully Jess heard bedlam break out, as the winning horse passed under the wire, saw the winning cowgirl acknowledge the ovation they gave her, and the track being cleared. Then, while dust settled to dust, over the vast assemblage a hush fell.

"Ladies and gentlemen," boomed the man with the megaphone. "Nex' event is the buckin' horse contest for the championship of Big. . . ."

A roar from thousands of throats and wild hubbub. For now the range was divided against itself. Every Big Smoky man, woman, and child had picked a favorite son to win. From friendship, kinship, or plain policy, each had come to back his choice to the extreme limit of purse and lung.

"Five hundred bucks goes with the title," rolled from the megaphone over the grounds. "Whoever gets it . . . he'll earn it, folks! This is goin' to be a real contest. We've brought in some of the toughest buckers in the West. Some has never been rode, none intend to be. One has been the despair of a hundred riders, an' the death of one, just six weeks ago on the Chetah track. . . ."

"I know that baby . . . tough bronc'!" shouted a voice from the throng.

"Every name is known to fame! Cowboys, hear 'em an' weep . . . Loco, Last Laugh, Hay-Maker, Whiz-Bang, Fidgety Dan, an' the notorious man-killer, Hell-Gait!"

Enthusiastically they applauded that name, and wildly cheered the contestants, rushing to the stand to draw their mounts. As Jess had been last to enter, so he was last to draw his horse. His hands shook so that he could hardly open his slip. All about him the other boys were comparing theirs, thanking their stars, or bemoaning their luck. The more vicious the horse drawn, the luckier they considered themselves. For the chance that it could not be ridden was offset by the almost certain prospect of winning if it could.

"Last Laugh!" disgustedly snorted a pink-shirted waddy. "Aw, hell . . . an' I wanted to *ride!*"

"Not so bad . . . mine. Whiz-Bang," Chuck Saunders congratulated himself. "But who got Hell-Gait?"

They all wondered that, but nobody spoke.

"Speak up, you lucky stiff," urged Chuck.

In his elation, forgetting himself, Jess said eagerly, as he held out his slip: "I did."

He remembered, then, with searing humiliation, just who he was, and what. For they stared right through him — these boys who had gone to school with him — till Chuck put an end to it at awful length by grabbing the pink-shirted waddy, and hauling him around with: "Come on, Dave . . . you open the show."

They moved toward the chute. Jess, trailing behind, could not help hearing Chuck's bitter complaint: "I'd 'a' give my eyeteeth to have drawed that hoss." And he was not spared Dave's fervent: "So say we all! But the devil sure looks out for his own."

Jess stumbled, half blind. But resolutely blinking the blindness away, he stopped by his horse, and stripped the pathetic old saddle off, then waited with what patience he could for his name to be called, hearing, above the crowd's loud rumble, the loud voice of Met Fergus, directing the saddling of the first outlaw. Then came the announcer's bawl: "First rider, Dave Martin, of the S Three Bar, on Last Laugh!"

To the frantic cheers of his friends, Dave climbed the fence. Followed a few seconds of frenzied finance, as bets were laid down and snapped up again, then Dave, jauntily waving his sombrero, eased into the saddle. The blindfold was jerked off, the gate swung, and Last Laugh shot onto the track. But Dave's adherents had barely time to see that he was aboard, when he was spinning over the outlaw's head. Even as he picked himself out of the dust to wave at the grandstand with a foolish grin and groggily limp back to the chute, the next contestant was called: " 'Coot' Hall, of the Triple Dot, on Fidgety Dan!"

Coot climbed the fence to the rousing cheers of his partisans, who as feverishly gambled on him. Odds rose, as Fidgety Dan plowed up the dust before the grandstand, and Coot sat him through several terrific bucks. Then, to the groans of his backers and the jeers of the others, he, like Dave, bit the dust.

"Chuck Saunders, of the Ace of Clubs, on Whiz-Bang!"

A storm of cheers greeted Chuck's appearance on the fence, for the Saunders family stood high in the range, and, as Ford predicted, human nature was working overtime. The cheer rose to a roar, as Chuck was catapulted out of the chute, and Whiz-Bang went weaving, sunfishing, bucking, all over the track with Chuck sticking like a burr, slapping his sombrero about Whiz-Bang's ears at every jump.

"That's ridin'!" yelled a man who had every cent in his pockets on Chuck.

"Stay with him!" shouted another in the same plight.

"Ya-a-ah! Boy, you got 'im!"

Chuck was still aboard when the whistle blew for the pick-up man to lift him off. This was done to a veritable thunder of applause.

"Mint Wade, of the Fiddleback, on Loco!"

One by one, like the roll of fate, names were called, and their owners rode, inexorably nearing the moment when Jess's name would be put to the test. What if Hell-Gait threw him, relieving Jim Fergus of all necessity of sitting in judgment on him? A probability that Jess did not even consider. He was as sure he could ride the killer as he was certain of putting up a better ride than Chuck, who he saw as his only competitor.

He watched Mint climb the fence to the cheers of his friends. Cheers sure helped. Let you know folks was back of you. He'd sure be mighty proud when. . . . Slowly and sickeningly, the boy's heart turned in his breast. They wouldn't cheer for him — not for a Trailor. Panic seized him, horror of the moment when his name was called. Vividly he pictured himself mounting that fence in dead silence, in shameful contrast to the reception accorded every other rider. It did not seem as though he could bear it. He wanted to run — bolt from the grounds.

But corral men were hazing Hell-Gait into the chute,

handling him with the utmost respect, holding him with taut ropes, while they prodded him along through the bars. Hell-Gait, the Waterloo of a hundred riders, and the death of one. A great, red-eyed, red-skinned demon of a horse.

While the crowd roared at the short, sweet battle between Loco and Mint, Jess carried his old saddle up to the fence and handed it to Met Fergus, bold-eyed, blond, and insolent, so surprising Met by his presence there that he accepted the saddle without comment. But, as Jess turned to look at his horse, he heard a jeering laugh above, and Met's lordly voice: "Hey, boys! Here's the saddle Ol' Man Noah rode onto the Ark!"

It looked so likely, as Met held it out, that everyone laughed. Encouraged by that: "Say, Trailor," Met bawled, "I'd have thought you could have rustled a better saddle than that."

Every eye turned on Jess, for Met's inflection made that remark an open insult. But there was no sign the boy took it as such, except a burning look in his eyes that awed Met into saying, more civilly: "It'll last quick on Hell-Gait."

Jess answered him quietly. "It'll last longer if I put it on myself. I'll saddle my own horse."

Taking old three-in-one from Jim Fergus's son, Jess dropped it on Hell-Gait's twitching back, cinched it carefully there, while men still held the blindfolded brute, and carefully inspected every part. Then he stood back, outwardly cool, but in actual torment, as cheers for Mint subsided to deepen the hostile silence that would greet him. He waited slow ages of torture in which the announcer lifted the megaphone to his lips, and curtly — coldly, it seemed to Jess — announced the last rider: "Jess Trailor, on Hell-Gait!"

The crowd's acclaim for the ill-famed horse was strangled in outrage at his rider's identity. So, as, mechanically, Jess climbed the fence, there fell the silence he had dreaded — a ghastly, hate-filled silence, that deafened him, smothered him, took all the confidence, the heart right out of him, and he wished the ground would open up and swallow him. That silence lasted while a brand-new pulse in his throat set up a furious throbbing; so long, that he could have counted each face in the multitude of faces before him; so still, that he heard the hoarse breathing of the killer below him.

And then — incredible joy shot through him. His heart lifted. His glowing eyes sought that for which all eyes were seeking — Met Fergus, cursing by the fence; Jim Fergus, rearing up in the judges' stand to see if what his outraged ears told him was true; the great crowd, straining, craning, fighting to see the person who dared to publicly cheer Jess Trailor.

They saw no stranger, as they had expected, but one of Big Smoky's own. A slender, vibrant, black-eyed girl, prettier than any picture, in scarlet blouse and short, fringed skirt. A girl who stood out from them all at the grandstand rail, waving her white sombrero, and cheering, in defiance of the crowd: "Ride him, Jess!"

Exaltation sang in the boy's veins. Oh, he could ride Hell-Gait — anything — with Jetta back of him, standing up for him. She wasn't changed — or ashamed.

Jauntily, as any rider there, Jess waved his shapeless hat to her. He dropped to the killer's back and, signaling the gateman, sang out with fine disdain: "Let 'er buck!"

IV
" 'A COLD-BLOODED FREEZE-OUT!' "

Oh, Big Smoky had to watch Jess Trailor. Eyes could not look through and not see. Eyes had not the power to turn away. They had to watch and, watching, forget for moments together that he was not a favorite son — but the son of Ute Trailor.

Jess had given the word. The blindfold was whipped off. Ropes were loosed. The gate swung. With a blood-curdling scream, Hell-Gait launched his thirteen hundred pounds of quivering fury into the arena, snapping into the vicious, double-headed buck that had lost a hundred riders their seats and killed one. It was a buck that brought the crowd to its feet. The great, red brute seemed simultaneously to hurl himself high in the air and whirl, changing ends as he landed with a frightful *thud* on all four hoofs. Then bawling, baffled fury, as for the first time this trick failed, he tried it again and again, while the boy on his back goaded him, fanning his ears with the old hat, his spurs flashing to the outlaw's shoulders at every jump.

Abandoning this method, as his satanic brain devised a new murder plan, Hell-Gait summoned all his brute strength and began back-jumping with a force and fury calculated to dislodge anything from his back. It seemed that no rider on earth could sit it out. It brought despair even to Jess, until over the pound of hoofs, the roar of blood in his head, cut that shrill, girlish cheer: "Jess, you ride him! I'm with you, Jess!"

Jetta was with him. What mattered those against him. Jess rallied to ride. Although the killer sunfished until the boy's boot heel touched earth; although he pitched in terrible snaps, when it seemed that the intrepid rider had not a chance to escape being thrown and kicked to death; although he spun and spun, till the watchers dizzied, and they, the blue sky, the yellow earth, were an indistinguishable blur to Jess. . . .

"You ride him!" she cried.

And Jess rode! He rode until the audience gasped, straining for glimpses of his white face through the swirling red tail and mane, the all-enveloping dust. Even the Ferguses, father and son, who most hated him, must watch and hate him more bitterly in their chagrin. From corral tops, spellbound, they watched — these boys who had gone to school with him. While a lone voice cheered, they watched Jess ride, and an official-looking stranger in the grandstand hoarsely besought his neighbor: "Who is that nervy kid?"

"A two-legged skunk!" The Big Smoky man just remembered. "One of the cow thieves who are stealin' us blind. Nervy . . . yeah. To be here . . . ridin' ag'in' decent men. He's a Trailor. We got his father an' brother . . . an' we'll get him in time."

"You mean," with fresh interest pressed his inquisitor, "he's the son of Ute Trailor, the rustler killed here last fall?"

Savagely the Big Smoky man retorted: "That's what I mean!"

"But are you sure this lad's a rustler?"

"Waal," was the sarcastic answer, "he may be livin' on heavenly manna, but if I lose many more cows, I'll be needin' a little of that myself. A rustler? He couldn't be anything else with that blood."

"Or with that feeling against him," said the stranger grimly.

"What's that you said?" sharply demanded the Big Smoky man.

But the authoritative stranger was staring in horror at the impending tragedy on the track. And horror was in the dark eyes of the girl who had long ceased to cheer, but gripped the rail with a frantic prayer. For the red, rearing beast was toppling back, back — deliberately throwing himself over to crush his rider. They saw Jess's legs twist, his spurs savagely rake at the killer's flank, bringing him down in the very nick of time to save himself from a horrible death.

Then, bellowing his rage, the thwarted horse pitted his unlimited strength against the boy's power to endure, leaping straight up and down unceasingly; awful, stiff-legged bucks, that brought blood trickling from the boy's nostrils and ears; terrible jars, that no flesh and blood could long bear, but which Jess must bear, so he would not have to go on alone, so he could be a man among men — *honest* men — jars that seemed tearing muscle from bone, but which he must stand, so folks would not keep tearing the heart right out of him; killing shocks that he must take in order that his life might be free from the kind of shocks he had got when they brought his father home to him — and the night he had found Dan.

Fogging pain made all dim and unreal but the stakes he was fighting for. He could not lose — now he had seen Jetta again. He could not go Trailor — and shame her for what she had done for him. He must just ride — everything came to an end some time. Just take that *thud, thud, thud,* and hold together.

Then, to the relief of everyone, the whistle was blown. The first time a whistle had ever been blown for a rider on Hell-Gait. The pick-up galloped alongside to lift Jess from the horse, but, weakly, the boy waved him back. He must not stop — Hell-Gait must stop. There must not be any doubt. He must ride to a finish — so Jim Fergus could not help but give him the prize.

To Jim Fergus's great satisfaction, Jess did. Although he remembered little more of that ride, only knew, after an eternity of torture, that the horse had stopped bucking.

Painfully, then, he got down, and, somehow, to the fence. He hung to it, dusty, dazed, and bloody, until things quit going around, hearing, as he wiped dust and blood from his face — cheers! Far-sounding, through the roar in his head, faint and few, but wonderful as celestial music — cheers for him! They made him strong. Folks would have to be a little proud of him now — champion rider of Big Smoky range.

Drawing himself up, Jess looked across to the judges' box. All three men were waving their arms, arguing — why, there was not any argument. No — for even Jim Fergus nodded assent. Now, as the announcer stepped out in front, lifting the megaphone, Jess did not dread hearing his name. This time he could not wait.

"Ladies and gentlemen," — oh, why go through all that red tape — "the judges have found it hard to reach a decision." What was hard about it — giving it to a Trailor? "You have just witnessed a remarkable ride, but" — no buts about it — "the judges regret" — oh, sure, they'd regret it, but they would have to, wouldn't they? — "that they are forced to disqualify Jess Trailor. He ignored the signal, an' refused to be taken from his horse. Therefore, they have no recourse but to award the prize to the next best rider, Chuck Saunders, of the Ace of Clubs."

Rare, unconscious tribute to Jess, the long, long silence that fell then, for the crowd was stunned by the verdict. At last Chuck's admirers set up a cheer, and others, recov-

ering, joined in, glad to see the highest honor in their power
to bestow go to anyone but a Trailor. The rest, thinking,
perhaps, that Jess had been fairly discriminated against, reluctantly added their plaudits for Chuck.

But, here and there, as love of fair play triumphed over
hate for the rustling Trailors, a voice rose hot against the
decision.

"Rotten!"

"A cold-blooded freeze-out!"

"Contest . . . bah! The rawest deal I ever saw pulled off
on this . . . or any track!"

But cheers, jeers, all were alike to Jess, standing by the
fence, white, stricken, like a man slowly bleeding to death.
One thought cut through the whirl in his brain — they
would not have dared hand out that deal to his father, Ute
Trailor.

All of him seemed, then, to die but his eyes — his al-
mond-shaped eyes. They lived — were intensely alive, with
blue fire. His head came up higher. His shoulders set
straighter. Before them all, the boy of the cañon changed
sinisterly, subtly — he was now all Trailor. Things did not
hurt — any more than the rain had hurt Dan that night. In
fact, he had a sense of relief, as of long strain over. He was
done with a losing battle. They had repudiated him. Now
he would have the game with the name. They would have
the respect of fear for him — which Ford had said was
something. He was deaf to the great buzzing that went on
about him. He had come to the end of his blind alley, and
Ford was there — up on the Little Jack Pine, waiting.

Indifferent to the curious eyes upon him, Jess crossed
the track, and took his saddle from the rider who had re-
trieved it from the outlaw's back. Then he hunted up
Bucky, and was cinching it on, when the boys reached him.

"A danged shame, Jess!" Chuck cried, in that tone of companionship for which Jess had once hungered.

But, without a word, he turned from these waddies who would have consoled him, mounted, and rode down the track to the judges' box. Jim Fergus was coming down the steps. But Jess swung his horse broadside, barring his path.

"Fergus," the boy's blazing eyes underscored the threat in his cryptic speech, "for this . . . an' other things . . . I'll pay you back."

Leaving the rancher choking with wrath, he whirled and deliberately rode over to the grandstand rail, where the scarlet-bloused girl waited in suspense. Before her, before them all, Jess dismounted, and swept off his hat. His face was totally devoid of color, but there was about him, more markedly than ever, that something that made him different, compelling — all that unusual strength of body and spirit, unleashed now that the course of his life was decided.

"Thanks, girl," he said to her alone, "for what you done. It wasn't the first time. I ain't forgot that old time."

Her black eyes haunted his, and her hand fluttered to her throat. "Jess," she said.

So for the first time since childhood they met, man and woman, with the old attraction fusing into something beautiful and deathless between them.

"It ain't likely," Jess said tensely, "that I can ever do anything for you. But if ever I can . . . Jetta, I'd give you the linin' of my heart for moccasins."

She cried, oblivious of prying ears and eyes: "Oh, Jess, you look so . . . I'm afraid of you, of what you'll do! Don't let this embitter you, Jess. It just goes to prove you'll have to leave here . . . go away. Go so far nobody will know, or care, who you are."

He said simply: "It's a day too late for that."

Then he rode to the watering trough just beyond, where he heard Met Fergus loudly upholding his father's decision to Spike Travis and some other Seven Star men.

At any other time Jess would have waited till he came to the creek just outside the gate to water his horse. But not this new Jess. Swerving sharply, he rode up to the trough, crowded back the nearest horse, and, getting down, slipped Bucky's bridle. Then he stood back, waiting for him to drink, and saw Met's eyes fall on him, as he knew they would, with an ugly gleam.

"See here, Trailor," bawled the Seven Star son and heir, wedging through to Jess. "I saw you talkin' to Jetta. I won't stand for any low-down son of a rustler makin' up to my sister. You steer a wide path around her from now on . . . savvy?"

For once in his life, Jess answered Met as he wanted to, not in word, but act — an act swift as lightning, and as unexpected. In an amazing burst of strength, he seized the bull, by shoulder and waist, lifted him high, and plunged him head first into the watering trough. Then he waited coolly by, until Met scrambled out, sputtering, amid water and oaths. "You . . . you. . . ."

"Don't say it, Met."

There was that in Jess's low-voiced command, his smoldering glance that made Met afraid to. Nor had anyone else a word to say, although Jess looked hard at Spike Travis and each Seven Star man. Then, leisurely mounting, he rode away, just as the official-looking stranger who had evinced such interest in him in the grandstand pushed through.

"Where's young Trailor?" the newcomer demanded of Met, who stood open-mouthed still, dripping wet, an ungodly halo of green scum and water weeds on his blond head. "I thought I saw him come this way. Did you see him?"

Somebody tittered. Met glared. But an accommodating bystander promptly answered: "Just left, stranger. Take my hoss, here, you can catch him before he leaves the grounds."

But it was hours before the obliging waddy got his horse back. For the stranger, overtaking Jess, had ridden with him, questioning, probing him, shrewdly sounding him out. At last — when it was a day too late — Jess was offered a job. He could not take it — now that he was a Trailor.

He rode alone into the crimson sunset, where, high up in one of the timbered notches, the Little Jack Pine flowed, and Ford Cruze waited.

V
"THE RUSTLING TRAIL"

Up on Ford's place, the endless rest of that September. Rest, while the last leaf fell, withered and sere, and to naked whips of brush clung the red berry of the mountain ash and white snowberry, while the wild geese flew over with high honking, and, in every desolate grove, birds assembled for southern migration, while cattle losses drove Big Smoky ranchers to desperation.

Up on Ford's place, nothing was like Jess had expected, but much the same as in his own blue cañon. It might have been his own place lifted high in the mountains, except for the presence of Ford, and of Bart and Seminole — two gaunt old range wolves, who had ridden with his father. Just another such an unkempt, run-down litter of buildings and corrals and insecure pastures of wild sod that had never felt plow, or burgeoned a harvest.

A horse ranch, Ford called it, and got away with it because of the small band of fast, blooded saddle stock that he ranged on it; because it was so far from anyone, so hard to get to, that few ever came to it; because Ford could get away with anything — could tell you that the moon was made of green cheese, and you'd believe it, or, anyhow, believe that *he* believed it. Just as he got away with his rustling for years and was not suspected as much as men who were straight because he looked like anything but what he was with his honest, cinnamon face — the old rustler.

Up on Ford's place, Jess was crazy for action. Crazy to rustle every cow in the country, starve out every rancher, beginning with Fergus. With the old-new, devastatingly hopeless worship for Jetta, crazy to plunge so deep into iniquity that he would have to forget her, have to put out of his heart forever something she had put into with that flattering "Jess!" As her eyes haunted his, then and thereafter, he had some crazy idea that if he had gone away, and made good, someday. . . .

Up on Ford's place, Jess was wild to be a holy terror — show folks it wasn't safe to hand out that deal to a Trailor. Yet, he was idle, committing no sin to collect wages on, making no money, easy or otherwise, still wearing the old clothes, more out at the elbow than ever, still riding old three-in-one, but wearing, too, Ute Trailor's old guns. Jess was wearing himself out — waiting, burning himself out — remembering, breaking horses for Ford to kill time, and feeling himself breaking, feeling things closing in — dreadful things, that were closing.

Even Ford's welcome had been disappointing. The old rustler had been glad to see him, and fighting mad at the way they had treated him, although it was just what he had expected. But, considering that for a whole year he had begged him to join the gang, Ford might have shown a little enthusiasm. Jess got the impression that the old fellow was none too happy about his coming, and saw how Ford kept putting him off from day to day, when he begged to accompany them.

Something had happened to Ford since that day he had ridden down to the cabin. He went around with a long face, and a deep crease between his eyes, like a man with a load on his mind. What was wrong, Jess wondered? Why didn't Ford tell him?

He had wondered, too, breaking horses for Ford to kill time, where Ford's gang was, and why it wasn't mentioned. He was greatly surprised to learn that this was the size of it. How could Bart and Seminole and Ford get away with stolen cows on the wholesale scale with which they had been disappearing on Big Smoky? How did they work, anyway? Where did they ride off to every day, coming in at all hours, with themselves in a stew and their horses all lathered? Why didn't they take him?

"You kept at me to join," impetuously he broke out on Ford one night, when the old fellow rode in alone. "Now I'm in. Put me to work. Name how many cows you want, an' I'll rustle 'em."

Ford's weary face had lighted with a smile at his fervor. "Now I know you're a Trailor. You sound just like Ute. That was his style, an' Dan's . . . ride down an' rustle. But times have changed. With ranchers on the look-out, like they be, we wouldn't last two days workin' that-a-way."

"How do you work?" Eagerly Jess seized this opening. While, still undisturbed, they had supper together, and Ford told him.

"Son, there's rustlers an' rustlers. Ute was a raider. I'm

what you might call a trader. His way was quick, but too risky. But I've worked out a scheme that adds considerable to the longevity of the profession. I picked out a man I could trust an' planted him down on the range. For ten dollars a head, he delivers cattle to a certain place. I don't know where he gets 'em. The brands they wear don't belong to any rancher in Big Smoky . . . an' I ain't supposed to ask are they worked over. I take 'em to a safe place in the hills till I can sell 'em to buyers who ain't no more curious about brands than me. I'm the middle man, see? The man I buy from. . . ."

Into Jess's mind flashed the image of a wizened, coyote face, and he cried: "That's Spike Travis!"

Ford's eyes met his hard. "How'd you know, Jess?" he asked.

"Just guessed."

"Waal," Ford admitted, "between us two, you hit the nail on the head. Spike's in on the ground floor. Workin' for Fergus, he ain't suspected. I picked him because he looks so simple, but he ain't nigh so simple as he looks."

Jess did not doubt that. "Does Spike know I'm here?" he asked.

"Nobody does . . . but Bart an' Seminole, an' you can trust them."

"Which I sure don't Spike." The boy's eyes flashed his dislike.

Ford nodded. He did not blame Jess. He had a better understanding of the old grudge Spike bore the Trailors than ever Jess had. Ford believed that old feud had died with Ute. But he was glad he had not said anything about Jess to Spike.

"What I don't savvy," Jess mused, "is how you can operate on such a scale, with only one man. . . ."

139

"Holy smoke, son! You don't think we're gettin' away with all the cattle that's missin' around here."

Blankly Jess stared at him. "Who is, then?"

The old rustler cried feelingly: "I wisht I knew!"

This conversation gave the boy something to think about and help to kill time. For, as the days passed, Ford still kept him champing the bit, almost beside himself with impatience. Each day deepened the crease between Ford's eyes. His shoulders settled, as if with the weight of a nation. Jess knew from the talk, that ranchers were making the range hot. He began to think that Ford was holding him back, so he would be out of the crash that was bound to come. And he did not like that. If his friend was in trouble. . . .

"Ford," he pleaded, dropping down on the porch beside him one day, "what's on your mind?"

He expected only evasions, and was dumbfounded when the old fellow flared: "Rustlers, damn 'em! There's too damned many of 'em. They're drivin' us ol' vets out of the business. An' the low-down, thievin' lay-out is rustlin' my cows."

"Your cows!" the boy gasped.

"Cows that I bought. . . ."

"At ten a head?" interjected Jess, grinning.

"Which sure counts up," declared the outraged old rustler. "They've about cleaned me out."

"You mean" — it made Jess somewhat dizzy to follow — "that the other rustlers are actually rustlin' the cows you rustled?"

"The cows which I bought from Spike." Ford was explicit. "Son, the last three herds have plumb disappeared. My safe cattle cache . . . safe! . . . they found it . . . cleaned me out. But" — and his eyes blazed with indignation, his voice shook with it — "if ever I find the two-legged coyotes what stole my cows. . . ."

It was too much for Jess, and he burst into a ringing laugh. It was funny to hear Ford cussing rustlers like a regular rancher, as mad at the idea of somebody stealing cows he had taken as even Jim Fergus could be.

"It ain't just their stealin'," Ford pointed out glumly, "they're overdoin' it. What I swiped ain't a drop in the bucket. An' the way we do, a rancher can still make a profit. But this gang is bleedin' the range. I hear Fergus ripped Sheriff Carey right up the back, an' that Carey's imported outside help. Already, there's deputies sproutin' in every bush. Son, the man takes his life in his hands who rides down the range of nights."

"Is that," Jess asked steadily, "why you're makin' sure I don't ride down?"

Ford's eyes fell from the direct gaze of Jess Trailor. "I . . . ," he began. Then abruptly: "Jess, is them the best boots you got?"

The boy looked down, his face flushing hot. But he said honestly: "They're all I got."

"Great snakes!" Ford was overcome with remorse. "Here I planned to do so much for you . . . an' I let you go barefoot." He went down in his chaps and dug up a roll of bills that he tossed to Jess. There was fifty dollars. But Jess handed it back.

"Not when you're short, Ford."

"Short?" Ford chuckled. "Son, you can't keep a good man down. I'll have plenty tomorrow."

But as much as Jess needed the money, he could not accept.

"I ain't earned it." He stuck to that.

"You will . . . before you have a chance to spend it," was the thrilling promise.

Wildfire swept the boy's soul. "Then I'm goin' to ride?" His dark eyes glowed.

"Tonight." Necessity, only, dragged the reluctant words from Ford. "I've scraped up money to buy a new herd. I'm to meet it at dark, an' I need you to help me get it to the hills. I got a new hidin' place, an' I aim to make it safe by ridin' herd on them cows with a gun till I sell 'em."

They sat in silence together, each busy with his own thoughts, until the two old wolves hove in sight on the trail, and Jess inquired: "Is Bart an' Seminole goin' to help?"

"You bet. We wouldn't get far without their help. They cover trail. Why, they're the only reason we ain't been tracked down . . . so far." Ford gave the porch rail a tap with his knuckles by way of "knocking wood" and so propitiating the gods. "They work alone. Tonight when we slip the herd away, they'll drop in behind with a bunch of range cows they've gathered up in the neighborhood an' follow us to the ford, blottin' out our tracks. We drive into the river an' through the gorge, while they just drive in an' out on the opposite bank. So any Sherlockin' waddy on the scent don't notice that there was twice as many cows went into the water as what came out, an' he keeps on the trail of them cows till he finds 'em grazin' peaceful somewhere, allows they're just strays, an' he's got on the wrong trail."

Jess was more impatient than any of them for night to come. As day waned, he was as restless and strung as a soldier on the eve of battle. Well might it be battle. Big Smoky cowmen were as apt to strike at any move, any sound, as a skin-shedding rattler. Up on Ford's place, all were preparing for battle.

Guns were cleaned, oiled, and tried. Jess, with the rest, cleaned, oiled, and tried the old guns of his father, nervously wondering if he would be the dead shot he had always been, if he had occasion to use them tonight. It was one thing to put a gun in shape to hunt game for a living, and another to test it out with the thought that man might be the next game sighted on.

He was relieved to see that his nervousness was shared by the three old veterans. They grew moody, morose, as the sun sank. Supper was got through without an unnecessary word being said. In silence, soon after, Bart and Seminole took their departure.

As for Ford, Jess hardly knew him. Now, with the time for action nearing, Ford looked what he was — a rustler. All his good humor had been put off like a mask. Under it, his face was stern, his eyes like granite. His easy-going demeanor became one of grim purpose. It occurred to Jess that Ford might have gone far had he turned his talent into legitimate channels. For it took brains to handle three units of men, each working independently of the other.

With a glance at his watch, Ford went outside, and Jess followed. The purple shadows of the Big Smokies were on the plains that spread so far below into infinity. Together the men saddled the blaze-faced black, and Ford mounted.

"Wait here an hour," he bade Jess, "no more an' no less. Then take the trail down the ridge past your place till you come to Hangman Creek. I'll be there with the cattle."

He rode off through the stunted jack pines. Jess followed him with his eyes until Blaze's black legs disappeared and the little trees came together.

I shouldn't 'a' watched him out of sight, he worried, *they say it's bad luck.*

He grinned at the fancy. But, as blacker and blacker fell the shadows about him, more deeply dark — waiting his hour out by his saddled horse — fell the black shadow across the boy's heart. A premonition of worse than bad luck. In it fear had no part.

VI
" 'YOU'RE WANTED . . . PRONTO!' "

Night fell like a blanket spread over the trees as Jess rode down the ridges, coming out on the rim above his own little cañon. His straining gaze picked out his cabin down there in the dark, forsaken. A pang pierced his heart. After all, it was home, and his memories of it weren't all unhappy.

There had been kid days, when he and Dan had played here like any boys, whooping it up until the very rocks rang, nights, when the cabin was filled with wild company — his father's friends. He and Dan had sat at their feet as they grouped by the fire, drinking in their tales of high adventure, tales that held glamour then, that had "got" Dan, and would have claimed Jess, but for Jetta.

"He can't help what his folks do!" Vividly, as on that night before his game ride, Jess saw her — a child — staunchly defending him.

"I'm with you, Jess!" Oh, so cruelly plain, he saw her — a woman — standing out at the grandstand rail, telling Big Smoky range she was with him. With him — on his way to rustle. That's how he was paying her back. For Jetta would pay. They would see she never heard the last of it.

Savagely he spurred Bucky, crazy to make the plunge and get it over. With him rode that foreboding of trouble. Ford had said that a man took his life in his hands who rode down the range at night. Yet the boy, riding down, had no sense of personal danger. Nevertheless, when the buckskin

144

came out of the timber at last, where it was lighter, Jess rode the harder.

Pulling up on a rise above Hangman Creek, he looked far down into the gorge, and saw the dull gleam of water. A full moon, rising, cast its radiance before him, and by its light Jess saw with a thrill a dark mass of moving backs — the cattle! Intently he scanned the scene for some glimpse of Ford on the flanks of the herd, but saw nothing of him, or thought more about it. Naturally Ford wouldn't be out where he could be seen.

But halfway down the steep trail, he lost sight of the river, and a queer impatience came upon him, a feeling that he could not get down there fast enough, an unreasonable anger, as he found his way barred by a fallen tree, lodged too high to leap, too low to get under. He lost moments that he somehow knew to be precious while Bucky fought the dense undergrowth, getting around it. Now, as he made it, Jess heard the first evidence of that danger of which instinct warned him — the bawls of suddenly frightened cattle.

With chilling fear that was not for himself, Jess crashed through the brush to the edge of the gorge, upreared his horse, and jerked back to shelter. For down there on the flank of the herd, struggling in the water, he had seen a man. And that man was not Ford!

How he was so sure of that, with only a fleeting glimpse in the dark, Jess never knew. But he was. He got off his horse, worming his way like an Indian back to the brink. He was parting the low brush to look, when, over the bawls of the terrified herd, crashed a pistol shot! From somewhere down there, a faint cry of agony. *Crack! Crack! Crack!* Three more shots. In that split second, while an unseen finger still pressed the trigger, Jess was on Bucky, recklessly racing down the slope to the river level, well knowing what it meant for him, a Trailor, to be seen near rustled stock, and not caring. He was a rustler now, and Ford was his partner. In that wild plunge down the bank, he jerked free his gun, and, as suddenly a galloping form loomed before him, determinedly he leveled it. But he did not shoot. For, as the animal neared, he saw the wild, swinging stirrups — Blaze, Ford's horse — riderless.

Quicker than thought, he wheeled and cornered the runaway, managing to seize the reins as the snorting horse plunged before him. Then, leading him, Jess rounded a bend, and came suddenly upon the cattle.

They had stopped, were milling midstream, churning, bellowing. Jess jerked back in the brush of the bank, as a rider ahead splashed into the water, firing across their faces, wildly yelling, deliberately stampeding them back. A rider who turned so that the moon fell fully upon his face, giving Jess a brief, unforgettable glimpse of Met Fergus.

He thought, his heart leaping with hot hate, that Seven Star riders had trailed the stolen stock, surprised Ford, killed him, and were taking the cattle back. The shock of that, the confusion, the dark, prevented his seeing who was riding with Met or how many, held him there in indecision while the cattle surged past, and the dark river rippled on its interrupted and melancholy song.

Then he set out to hunt for his friend, to hunt again, with that horrible ache in his breast, as on that night he had hunted Dan. He had thought then that such searches were over for him — that he had no more to lose. But, splashing downstream to where he judged the herd had been when he heard the first shot, Jess suddenly realized how much he loved Ford, how much there was about the old fellow to love. Ford's heart was as big as all outdoors, and he would stick by a friend through thick and thin.

Jess remembered with bursting heart — as he zigzagged his horse, to leave no hummock or swale of the rough bank unsearched — a thousand instances of Ford's kindness to him. There was no end to it — unless this was the end — no beginning that he could remember. He could remember being carried in Ford's strong arms when he was just a toddler. Ford had stood beside him, one arm about him, and one about Dan, when they buried his father. Ford's arm was about him when they laid Dan away. Ford had come back to the cabin afterward, so he wouldn't feel so lone. . . .

Bucky shied with a snort of terror, and the grieving boy knew his search was over. There lay Ford, stretched out in the dead leaves, his face to the stars.

Instantly Jess was down, bending over him, feeling his heart, feeling with horror, as his hand groped under Ford's buckskin vest, something warm, sticky, wet — feeling, too, joyfully, that heart's faint beating. Ford was not dead.

Frantically, then, in sudden dread of the riders' return, Jess tried to lead Blaze up. But the animal pitched and plunged and was so maddened by the smell of blood that he desisted. Blindfolding Bucky with his scarf, Jess succeeded, after a heroic struggle, in lifting Ford to his own saddle, and binding him there with his lariat.

Then, riding Blaze, and leading his sadly burdened pony, he set off at a slow pace up the steep trail home. Not to Ford's home, but to his own. He knew it meant conviction if the wounded man was found on his hands, but he did not care. Jess, too, stuck by his friends to the bitter end. His home was nearest, and Ford must have help.

Yet, in his anxiety, home seemed far to Jess. He thought he would never get to it. After he reached the cabin door, he thought he would never get Ford inside — he was so heavy — a dead weight. But Jess managed it somehow, and got him laid out on the bed. Then, by the flare of his smoky old lamp, he threw back Ford's vest, cut away his shirt, and gave first aid — skillfully, for he was practiced in treating such wounds, and had in fact dressed wounds much worse. For he found that the bullet had entered the body below the heart, passed through at an angle, and come out on the side. So that, when cold water and pain brought the old rustler to, and he gasped — "No stallin' . . . is it trail's end, Jess?" — the boy could tell him honestly: "It need not be. But," he huskily added, "I'd better get the doctor, Ford."

The ghost of a grin crossed the gray face then. "An' put a rope on my neck?" asked the old warrior. "No, son . . . I'll take my chances with you."

Then he must hear all that Jess had experienced. To quiet his mind, the boy told him how he had heard shots as he rode down, reaching the river just in time to see the Seven Star men turn back the cattle. . . .

"Seven Star men! How did you know?"

"I saw Met Fergus."

That had anything but a quieting influence on Ford. Intently he searched the face of Jess, who sat in a chair, bent over the bed.

"Son, are you sure it was Met?" he asked earnestly.

"Dead sure."

Jess wished Ford would not talk any more, although there were a number of things he was wondering himself. Did Ford know who had shot him? Had Bart and Seminole been caught? Were they lying out there under the stars, or hiding away in the hills — or what?

"Jess," feebly Ford cried, at a sudden thought, "you got to get me away from here. Things is goin' to pop. I won't have you blamed."

"Forget that, Ford. You stay here till you're well. Then we'll go back."

"No!" The old fellow's eyes filled with pain, not all due to his wound. "You must never go back. Son, it was fierce layin' there . . . oh, I lay awake a minute before things went black. An' I done more thinkin' in that minute, Jess, than in all the rest of my life. Son, I seen this way don't pay, either. Easy money! But it sure goes easy. Jess, your dad died broke. I'm broke, an' but for the mercy of heaven . . . dead."

"Don't, Ford." Tears stung the boy's eyes. "Rest."

But Ford could not rest. "Mebbe I got some sense shot into me . . . or conscience, Jess. But it's too late to do me any good. I'm mired too deep . . . to ever be rid of the mud. But you . . . you're just startin' out. An' I started you. That's been heavy over my head. I thought you was a fool to try an' live honest with things like they was, but when you come to me, I knew better. I've been sorry ever since, Jess. Like I was makin' a criminal out of my own flesh an' blood. . . ."

"Please, Ford."

"That's why I ain't let you ride before . . . an' I won't let you no more. Better starve honest, than lie in some hole . . . an' feel your life ooze out in the dark. I'm glad I got shot. If I hadn't 'a' been, you'd be a rustler now . . . an' past all help. But you can go on like you were here. Oh, I know you could live pure as an angel, an' they wouldn't believe. But, Jess, you would know. Nobody need know you was ever away from here, ever thought of bein' anything else. . . ."

"It's too late for me, too," said the boy brokenly. "I'll know, Ford."

"Too late for you?" Again that gray, ghostly grin. "Son, you talk like you was a hundred years old."

"I feel that way sometimes, Ford."

Then Ford, again scanning Jess, saw how tired he looked, burned up, charred. Something was wrong with the lad. He had been blind not to have seen it. His hand closed over Jess's upon the bed.

"Is there a girl, son?"

The boy's jaw quivered. "*She* don't know it."

"Is it Jetta Fergus," probed Ford in dread. Reading in the boy's tense face that it was, he turned away with a groan: "Heaven help you, Jess."

It was as if all the tragic presage of what was to happen filled the cabin.

Jess went outside and stabled the horses, and, when he came in, he thought Ford was sleeping. Careful not to wake him, he built a fire, wishing that he could tell Ford about the stranger. It might not be too late to take that job. But Ford had not really reformed — he had said it was too late for him. He was going on rustling. So he could not tell — he was on his honor.

"Put out the light." Ford was nervous, wide awake. "I feel queer . . . like there was prowlers about." Fretfully he said, as Jess plunged the room in gloom: "There's things goin' on which I don't savvy. Jess, why didn't they come back to see who they dropped? To see was I dead or not? They'd be more interested in catchin' a rustler . . . dead or alive . . . than in takin' the cattle. An' who are the other rust . . . ? What's that?"

It was hoof beats on the creek trail. Jess sprang up. "Seminole, mebbe," he whispered, "or Bart."

But Ford knew better. They would go home — they wouldn't think to come here. "No . . . it's the law. They trailed me. Boy, you let 'em take me. Hear? Say you ain't left this cabin tonight. Say I just crawled up here, an' you can. . . ."

But Jess had not heard a word. Snatching up a blanket, he spread it over his wounded friend, strung up another from the logs above, screening the bed. He pushed the basin and stained cloths under the bed, had wiped every sign of Ford out of the house, when a step sounded on the porch, a low rap on the door. Jess opened it, prepared to bluff it out, fight, anything but let them take Ford.

He was prepared for anyone but the one revealed by the flickering light from the fireplace on the curtain of night: the moist-eyed cowhand with the hangdog look and the limp Ute Trailor had given him. In his relief — for Jess had no thought but that Spike Travis had come to ask about Ford — Spike's amazing message was all but lost.

"You're wanted . . . *pronto!*" the Seven Star man jerked out. "You know that big standin' rock on the Salitas road . . . where the Seven Star road forks off?"

"I know. What about it? Who wants me?"

Fearfully, thick-tongued, as a Judas must have spoken, Spike made answer: "The Fergus girl."

VII
"TREACHERY"

"The Fergus girl," Spike repeated, wetting his lips as though the words parched them. "She says she wants to see you. She's waitin' at Standin' Rock."

With that off his chest — and what a weight it must have been — Spike backed off the porch. He was gone before Jess could collect his wits and question him. Dazed by the joyous wonder that Jetta had sent for him, the boy stared out into the empty night until the hoof beats died.

"Son, you ain't goin?" hoarsely whispered the wounded rustler.

"I got to, Ford." Jess went back to the bed. "Jetta wants to see me. She might need me. I hate leavin' you . . . but I won't be long."

"Forget me." Sturdily Ford dismissed that subject. "It's you I'm thinkin' of. Son, there's something fishy about all this. Spike ain't had time to go back to the ranch, get a message from Jetta, an' come clear up here since he turned the cattle over to me."

But Jess, hastily doing what he could for Ford's comfort in his absence, pointed out that Jetta might have given Spike the message before he left, or met him somewhere. Because this was possible, and on the slightest possibility the boy must go, the old fellow said nothing more to deter him.

"I'll be right back," Jess promised from the door — eager to go, Ford saw, but remorseful at leaving him here.

To send him away in an easier state of mind, Ford joked grimly: "Waal, I'll be here."

So, in that moment of parting, each unwittingly lied to the other. And for the second time that night Jess took the down trail.

It was not dark now. The moon rode high in a sky clouded only with stars, and a soft, white glow made the prairies almost like day. Swinging into the Salitas road, Jess could see Standing Rock, bulking black, far ahead. Nearing the giant boulder, his mind was harassed by its first real doubt.

He could not imagine a reason on earth why Jetta should want to see him, or why she might need him. Jim Fergus was as solid and prominent in Big Smoky as old Standing Rock. Jetta had him, her brother, the Seven Star crew —

yes, the whole range — to call on, if she needed help. She would not send for a Trailor.

Loping steadily to his spurs' soft jingle, he suspiciously recalled Spike's uneasy manner, his nervous haste to be off. Still, as a Seven Star man, he must have heard of the raid at the river, and, as the man who had rustled those cows in the first place, he would naturally be pretty scared. Spike hated him, and the feeling was mutual. But what object would he have in telling him Jetta wanted to see him if she did not? Spike would not dare to use her name without authority like that.

Nevertheless, his suspicion grew as he neared the rock. The Seven Star crew might have sent Spike up for a joke. No, he was not as important as that . . . to anyone but Met. Met Fergus would go a long way to get even for that public baptism in the watering trough. But he would not go about it as a joke.

All this time, his eyes had never left the rock, where Spike said Jetta waited. With caution born of his suspicion, he circled it to reconnoiter before riding up. His heart pounded as he saw something move in the shadow of the rock. The next instant he saw what it was — a coyote, that had been startled by his approach, and now went loping across the plains. It told him truer than words that Jetta was not here, or anyone.

Riding boldly up to the rock, Jess got down to study the ground about, noting the remains of a rabbit on which the coyote had been feasting when he had come along. It was freshly killed, proving that the animal had been hunting in this vicinity, and that no one had been here for some time. Nor did Jess find any fresh tracks. No woman's tracks at all. Jetta had not been here. But, for the life of him, Jess could not remember now whether Spike had said she was here or would meet him here. He decided to wait.

Leaning against the rock, the dense shade blotting out the outlines of himself and horse, Jess smoked a cigarette, his sight and hearing strained on the Seven Star road. He smoked another in his nervousness, as he waited a full thirty minutes, worrying over every moment he was away from Ford, thinking of a thousand things he might want and suffer for lack of, but unwilling to go while there was a chance of his being of assistance to the girl who held his wild heart captive.

In this period of forced inaction, Jess thought of a thousand reasons why Spike might have come to his cabin, and hit, at last, on one that seemed plausible. On hearing that a rustler had been shot at the river, Spike might have rushed to the aid of Ford, his partner, trailed him to the cabin, and, wanting to talk with him alone, invented the bogus message to get Jess away for a time. This explanation was so simple, so natural, that Jess was coming to accept it as truth, when he heard the beat of hoofs on the Seven Star road, not the beat of a lone horse, but of many horses.

Crouching in the shadows, holding Bucky's mouth and nostrils to repress a betraying snort or nicker, Jess saw a band of riders sweeping up in the moonlight toward the rock. He recognized Jim Fergus, with throbbing hate in every vein, and beside him a bulkier figure — Sheriff Carey of Salitas County, as he knew by the star that flashed. A posse! Going to search for the man the Seven Star crew had shot. They might trail Ford to the cabin. He must get back. And yet — Jetta.

In an agony of indecision, Jess stood there while the riders swerved into the hill road, passing out of hearing. Then he made up his mind. He would go to the Seven Star, three miles on, and try to see her. By riding hard, he could do that, and get back home before the posse would have given up search for the body, picked up the trail of Blaze and Bucky, and followed it to the cañon.

Accordingly he set off at a hard gallop for the Fergus ranch, with no more idea than the man in the moon of how he would see Jetta when he got there — at that hour, and without letting himself be seen.

But, racing along the willow-fringed road that bordered the Seven Star, and almost to the big gates, where he meant to hide his horse, a slender figure ran swiftly out of the gloom before him. Jess, standing in his stirrups as his horse reared, looked down into Jetta's lovely upturned face, filled with a wonder that matched his with nameless relief, fear — he knew not what.

With a sense of the miraculous strong upon him — that he should meet her thus on the public highway under a midnight sky — Jess slid down. Something electric there had always been between them and now drawn by that force — perhaps the force with which God ties His worlds — they moved together.

She spoke first, saying strangely: "I thought you were Met . . . coming back. He rode a buckskin, too."

Then, as their hands met and a long strain seemed broken with her voice catching at every word, she went on: "Thank heaven, you're here. Jess, there's something terrible going on."

Fearfully she looked about in the starry night. Jess felt her trembling. "I've been out here . . . waiting. I don't know for what. Jess, did you meet them?"

He knew she meant the posse and told her it had passed him at Standing Rock.

Again she cried: "Thank heaven!"

Presently as he waited, not daring to break the spell, not

daring to believe in the mad joy that possessed him, Jetta said: "Met rode home, all excited, about nine. Dad went crazy at some word he brought. They rounded up the neighbors . . . phoned the sheriff . . . and banded here. They wouldn't tell me what was up. But I heard your name and. . . ."

"It ain't me they want," tensely he told her. "I ain't done nothing to make them want me . . . yet."

That made stars of her eyes, brighter than any of heaven's stars. "Oh, don't ever, Jess. I've been so afraid . . . ever since the stampede. Afraid . . . of things that were in your face then. Don't ever do anything to make them want you. Promise, Jess?"

He could not promise, although that night Ford had begged him to, although Jetta begged him now, with trembling lips, with gleaming tears upon her lashes. The memory of that year-long fight was strong within him. His heart was still sore and sick from the blow Big Smoky range had dealt him.

"One man can't fight so many," he said slowly. "Some men might . . . but I can't. Maybe that's the Trailor in me. Anyhow, I ain't got the courage to go on alone."

She saw his face dark with pain and strain, as when he rode Hell-Gait. She guessed the lengths he might go to, as she had then, lengths to which, from things she had heard at home in the last few weeks, she had feared — until he told her now — that he had already done. She had seen him, a child, abused, but bravely holding up his head in the face of it. She saw him now, a man, accused, head still high, but his fiery eyes full of dangerous defiance. She thought of how he was the last of his name — and why — of the terrible grudge he must bear the community. She was brave enough to say, her black eyes on his: "You won't go on alone, Jess . . . I'll be with you. I'll find a way to help you. It's you and me against the rest of them, Jess."

She felt the yearning in his eyes, and her own response. Then she heard him crying, hoarse with pain, as he painfully crushed her hands in his: "You an' me, Jetta? That can't be. Heaven only knows what you've been to me. You'll always be that . . . an' more. But I can't take help from you. Not from a Fergus."

"Why?" she whispered, knowing why, almost afraid of him now — of the savage gleam in his burning eyes.

"Once," he said, in that strange, hoarse tone, "a posse rode away from here. Jim Fergus was in it. An' the man they wanted . . . an' got . . . was my dad." He went on — while she waited, in speechless horror at the thought that her father might have slain his father — "I'll do anything for you, girl. Let me prove it. Tell me what you sent for me to do . . . I came the minute you sent word."

She gave back a step in amazement.

"Sent for you?" she echoed wonderingly.

"Sent Spike Travis to tell me you'd meet me at Standin' Rock."

Yet a minute she stared up at him, knowing he spoke the truth, and finding in it vindication of her first alarm for him.

"Jess," she cried, seizing his arm, "I never sent Spike Travis . . . or anyone . . . for you."

Then Spike had wanted a talk with Ford, Jess thought. And this thought of Ford up there, helpless, while the posse searched. . . .

"Jess, go home . . . quick." Wildly, in an awful suspicion, she urged the thing he was wild to do.

He swung in the saddle. "*Adiós*, Jetta." He bent down. "If I can't do anything for you. ! . ."

"But you can." She swayed against him in her deep concern. "You can fight on. Something will turn up. You can hold out a little longer. Promise you will . . . for my sake. Say it, Jess."

"Oh, girl . . . a little longer . . . yes."

For her sake, he would. He meant it — burning up the dark road home. He would go back and get Ford away from the cabin in case the posse came there, and take care of him until he got well. Then he would live as he had before the stampede, or try to — honestly. He had not a cent to his name. This money in his pockets — this "easy" money — he would return to Ford. Thank God, he had not earned it tonight as Ford prophesied he would. But he took no credit to himself for that. It was not his fault he was not a rustler now, but an act of heaven. He would never forget that, in those weeks up on Ford's place, he had been a criminal in thought, if not in act.

Madly he rode, taking the hills at a run. Bucky was dripping foam when he turned into the cañon trail. Not once had Jess seen or heard a sign of anyone. Some of his anxiety departed, so that he let the pony set his own pace on the last steep stretch.

When he was actually in his cañon, and saw the little cabin ahead, all dark and quiet as he had left it, he could have sobbed in sheer relief. Never had home seemed so good. At a walk he passed beneath the cottonwoods, was almost abreast the corral when he pulled up sharply, and sat, staring, like a man turned to stone.

For that corral — idle all the year since Ute Trailor's death — was filled with stock. *Whose cattle were they*, wondered the astonished boy? *And how've they got into my corral?*

Still dumbfounded, he got off his horse, climbed the

fence, and went among them, stooping to make out the brands. A low cry of astonishment escaped him. They were the Ten Wheel brand. That was the brand Ford told him he had bought from Spike tonight.

Then these were the rustled cows that Ford had been driving when he was shot! The cows Met Fergus had stampeded back. Why had they brought them here? With trembling hands, Jess lit a match, and studied the brands. They had been worked over, and the work was crude and fresh. The Roman numeral ten had been a seven, and the wheel — the boy's blood chilled with a vague and terrible presage — the wheel was originally a star, but with a rude circle now burned about all points. They were Seven Star cows. Stock rustled from Jim Fergus in a Trailor corral. Stunned by the significance of that, Jess felt the prod of metal in his back, heard that grim command: "Hands up!"

Dazedly he obeyed, turning with a fatalistic sense of the inevitably of this, to see his captor, Sheriff Carey, to see also a grim and vengeful line-up of ranchers by the fence. Among them was the stranger — that gray, official-looking stranger, who had evinced such interest in Jess Trailor at the Stampede, but was now as hostile, implacable, as any man there.

"Admirin' your work, huh?" flamed Jim Fergus wrathfully. "It's nothing to be proud of, Trailor."

But the boy ignored him. "Sheriff," he said desperately, "there's something crooked here. I swear. . . ."

A loud laugh drowned him, loud and insolent, but shaken by strange agitation.

"Yeah?" Met Fergus swaggered forward. "We'll all swear to that. You two-bit rustler, we got you now."

They had "got" his father and brother, and, yes, they had him now. Jess realized it. But it was not of self he was

159

thinking then — only, and with agony, of Ford.

In the cabin, wounded unto death, lay the only friend he had on earth. These men could not have been in the cabin yet. He must let them take him — quickly — before they found Ford. It would mean years of prison for Ford, too — a death sentence. But, no, he could not leave Ford here to suffer and die alone. No one knew he was here — not even Spike. For Spike had just come to decoy him off, while they set this trap for him. Dully he heard the sheriff speaking.

"Trailor, I arrest you for the theft of these cows . . . Seven Star cows, as a blind man can see. Later, there'll be other charges."

Oh, sure, trumped-up charges like this. Wearily Jess extended his arms for the handcuffs, his lips trembling with what he must say.

"Whatever you say," the officer warned him, "may be used against you."

He said: "Can I go in the house first?"

They let him go — shackled, herded along by a dozen men, a dozen guns — to get, they thought, some clothing, some article he valued. But when he was inside, and the implacable stranger had found and lit the lamp at his direction they saw him stare blankly about. . . .

"Get what you want . . . an' get it quick," prompted the officer roughly.

But there was nothing that Jess wanted. For, climax to this night of climaxes — Ford was gone.

VIII
"FATHER AND DAUGHTER"

Big Smoky had him — the son of Trailor. The man who they believed had done the rustling. The man they had always suspected. They had him safely behind the bars of the Salitas County jail, his preliminary hearing over, awaiting trial. Jess was already tried and convicted in the public mind, with all the influence and affluence of Jim Fergus brought to bear against him, with everything against him, the circumstantial evidence, the unbeatable handicap of his hated name, the reputation they had given him, even his silence — for since the jail door had triumphantly clanged upon him, Jess had not said a word in his own defense. They had him. They were determined to make an example of him, and scare out his confederates, whoever they might be.

"Mebbe we'll get some peace then," was the grim comment of one cowman in the ever-changing, ever-present group that hung from dawn till dark outside the jail to discuss the capture. "It'll be the first time in my time that we ain't battened a Trailor."

"They'll put him where the dogs won't bite him," allowed a second. "His coyote blood will be tamed aplenty afore he gets out."

And a third put in: "He can thank his lucky stars I wasn't there. I'd have cast my vote for hemp."

Big Smoky was actually proud of its tolerance in not lynching Jess. A tolerance lamented by many of its citizens. Often the boy in his cell heard their voices raised against him in the street.

No one was allowed to see him. Jetta Fergus had tried, causing Big Smoky folks to gasp once more at her interest in a Trailor, but she had been refused admittance. Jim Fergus, hearing of it from Met, went wild.

Met had always been the child of his heart, the one on whom his pride and hopes had centered. He petted Jetta, was proud of her beauty, her popularity as it reflected credit on himself, but to him she was a little girl who had never grown up. Now he was to learn that she was a woman, with a mind and spirit of her own, to feel, in this crisis, that his daughter was a stranger to him.

"You're actin' plumb flighty over this Trailor cub," he charged her, going straight to her from Met. "I took you out of school here an' sent you off, so you wouldn't have to mix with such scum. An' you come back an' make a holy show of yourself at the Stampede. Not content to set every tongue waggin', you try to follow him to jail!"

She had been standing at the window when he entered, looking out over the range that loomed hauntingly, purple with the smoky haze of Indian summer. Now she turned and looked into his heated face, with nothing but heightened color to show she heard. She was still in her riding clothes as she had come from town, still with her black, bobbed hair windblown, but with something new in her bearing that struck through her father's anger, shaming him, warning him to adopt a more conciliatory tone.

"Reckon I can savvy, girl." Laying one hand on her bright hair, he placed the other under her chin, tilting her face up to him. "You see him as the underdog . . . gettin' the worst of it. You forget folks have a right to bait an' trap and spread poison for a wolf. You're a woman . . . an' you pity him."

He was taken aback by the vehemence with which she spoke then. "Pity Jess? No. Not more than I'd pity any man in his position. He doesn't need it. He's strong . . . stronger than you are, Dad. For you can't break him . . . not the whole range of you. You've accused him wrongly . . . in cowardly fashion. You've spread your poison. You've tried to starve him out. And now, everything else failing, you trap him. You sent Spike Travis up there, and got Jess away so you could put those cows in his corral. . . ."

"What's this?" cried Fergus sharply. "Spike? I put . . . girl, are you mad?"

"I will be . . ." — her voice broke — "with the thought that my own father helped condemn an innocent man."

Perplexed, he stared at her. "You think I framed him?" Harsh was that demand. "You think I'd do a trick like that?"

Her hand spread in a gesture, poignantly eloquent of her helpless state of mind. "I . . . don't . . . know," she said wearily. "I don't know what you wouldn't do . . . after the way you treated him at the Stampede."

He had the grace to flinch at that — a sore spot on his conscience yet. But he did not try to excuse or gloss over his conduct. He ignored it, as his mind leaped back to what she had said.

"Nobody framed him, girl. He was caught red-handed in the act. You was at the hearing. You heard the charge against him. You saw him sit an' sulk . . . too guilty to say a word for himself."

"What good would it have done?" she cried bitterly. "Who would have believed him? Don't you suppose Jess knew that?"

"There was nothing he could say!" The rancher's voice was rising with the ignominious suspicion that it was not pity alone his daughter felt for Jess Trailor, but that pity that is akin to love.

"Oh, yes, there was." White, unflinching, she stood up

to him. "He could have said that you went up there that night and put those cows in his corral while he was with me."

"You . . . ?" Fergus choked, staggered literally. Then, gripped by passion, changed almost beyond her recognition, he cried: "He was with you? You've met that *hombre* . . . on the sly. Girl, just how far has this thing gone?"

Her face lifted, and with no help from him. Her black eyes flashed a spirit that matched his own. But her tone was quiet, even appealed to him. "Dad, don't you know that Spike Travis went up there that night and told Jess I sent for him? No, I see you don't. But he did, Dad, and Jess came down here. We talked . . . I don't know how long . . . but quite a time. He knew a posse was riding at the time. Wouldn't he have rushed back to get rid of the evidence up there, if he had been guilty? Would he have stayed and talked to me? Won't a jury believe that false message has some bearing on the case?"

"No Big Smoky jury would believe Jess Trailor."

"But they will believe me," she cried ringingly. "I'll take the stand and swear it. I won't stand by and let them convict him for something he didn't do."

"An' I won't stand by an' see my family smirched!" her father thundered. "Folks will say. . . . You won't have a rag of reputation left. I'll spend my last cent to convict him, for what you've told me . . . if nothing else. He lied to you . . . trumped up that story . . . so he could drag you in as an alibi, an' shame me. But I'll squash that. Jetta, I forbid you to say one word of this!"

"Even if I could prove his innocence?" she whispered very low.

"Not if you could prove his innocence. There's enough

else he's guilty of. Men of his stripe deserve no mercy, an' he'll get none."

Fixedly she gazed at him, noting for the first time how hard the lines in which his strong, stern face were cast. Not a line of mercy in it. No, although ever so hard she searched for one. She came toward him slowly, making no move to touch him.

"Dad" — her voice had horror in it — "did you kill Ute Trailor?"

She thought he would never answer. The moment seemed endless, with nothing beyond it. She heard the nicker of a horse outside, the swish of the curtain breeze-blown against the vase of snowberries on the window ledge. She saw her father gather himself, seem to grow, to tower over her. . . .

"If I did," — and she would never have known that tone for his — "the score is paid. You forget poor Sidney . . . your cousin. Dan Trailor killed my only sister's son."

IX
" 'YOU'VE GOT TO GET ME OUT OF HERE!' "

In the hollow of his relentless hand, Jim Fergus held Jess Trailor. Fergus the man who most hated the Trailors, with most cause to hate. And the jailed boy knew that Fergus would never let him go. Already Jess felt that hand closing on him, crushing the life out of him. Already it had taken from him the one thing he had always had, nor valued when he had it — freedom, the one thing he could not live without.

What mattered it that men reviled him, persecuted him,

said all manner of evil against him falsely? What mattered it that hunger wore a familiar face, that he was condemned to solitary exile, or the fatal companionship of such men as Ford? What were such things compared to this?

The boy had grown up as free, as untrammeled, as any wild thing in Big Smoky's hills. Free to range the plain and forest as he willed, to breathe untainted air, to feel the sun. What loneliness had he ever known — with Bucky, who loved him, with living forests near him, and all the furred and feathered life that dwelt therein?

But here, in this dead place, where nothing was, not sun, not rain, not air a man could breathe, not space to move. He could not stand it here. And he had been here — how long? Three weeks. Waiting until they put him away, alive — for years — in another grave like this.

Nor could he do a thing to save himself. He could tell no part of the truth without incriminating Ford. Nor the whole truth without implicating Jetta. So he said nothing, and they held that against him.

To keep his mind from morbid imaginings over the fate of Ford, to live, somehow, this awful existence — broken only by two so-called meals a day and change of guard at night — Jess took up each thread of mystery and followed it as far as he might.

Why had no mention been made of the first raid, when Ford was shot? Who were the other rustlers who had cleaned Ford out? Could it have been they who planted the stolen stock in his corral? If not, who? Not Ford, even granting that he had been physically able to. Not Bart and Seminole — they might be cow thieves, but they were real old-timers, and incapable of double-crossing a friend. It must have been Spike Travis, who hated the Trailors, but. . . .

Every thread tangled on this hard knot. How had Spike got them from the Seven Star crew? Jess had seen the cattle himself since they had passed from Spike's hands to Ford's. He had seen them in the river being driven back by Seven Star men. But, he would ask himself, sitting on his cot, head in hands, his young face aged with the strain of such interrogation — did he *know* they were Seven Star men? Closing his eyes, he summoned to mind that night scene, when the herd churned in the stream, and a man fired across their faces, and he could see again the moonlit features of that man — Met Fergus, see the cattle surging back, and the river rippling on.

Met had been there — he could swear to that. But he did not know who had been with Met. He had supposed that they were Seven Star riders — supposed it yet. But, ransacking his mind in desperation, he could not actually recall having seen a single other man. Now remembering the cattle's actions, he was sure there must have been at least one rider on the opposite bank. Suppose — he snatched at every supposition — Met had planted the cows. What, then, of Spike? Then he would have to believe that Spike had decoyed him off so he could spirit Ford away, that there was no connection between the message and the Ten Wheel cows in his corral.

And if — starting on another thread — Spike, learning that Ford had come to grief, that Seven Star men had the cows, he had re-branded with that fatal Ten Wheel brand, had somehow got possession of them again, and, seeking to cast the blame on someone else, had driven them to Jess's corral — then what of Met? Spike could not have got them without Met's knowledge.

Always — although at times Jess felt maddeningly near the truth — there was that tangle.

Always, he thought of Jetta, of his promise to her. He had honestly meant to keep it, meant to tell Ford that night that he would live straight. Well, he would now — they would see to that. He lived over and over every moment of his meeting with Jetta, hungrily remembered her every word and glance. She had been afraid for him — had warned him — would have helped him. And her — "You and me against the rest." — would have made heaven of a cell for Jess.

But he reasoned himself out of that consolation. He had put meanings into her words she had not meant, given them intonations that had not been hers. He was so crazy about her, he had made himself believe she liked him, too. How could she — a girl like her. Because it was not right for him to love her, even to think about her here, he locked the door on love, as Big Smoky had locked freedom's door on him.

One night he stood before the little, high, barred window, looking out of his cage, looking up at his mountains, dark against the sky, waiting up there like faithful friends. They would wait for him. But he — could he stand it, shut away from them. A lump swelled in his throat. In his heart there grew a longing so intolerable that he could have thrown himself in futile rage against the bars. As it was now, so it would be — for years and years.

When, at last, worn out, he lay on his cot, tears were salt upon his lips. But he soon fell into a troubled sleep. He was roused toward dawn by a slight tapping, not loud enough to have aroused him had it been a legal sound, but its guilty insistence struck on his strung perceptions like a gong.

Tap! Tap!

Now he located it. Someone was tapping against his window bars. He strained his eyes on the black up there, his heart thumping painfully hard. For, through the bars — close-set in the concrete of the jail — he saw the dark outlines of a face, weirdly suspended in mid-air, for the window was fully ten feet from the ground, and the wall was sheer.

Rising noiselessly, he slipped to it, barely suppressing a joyous cry of recognition at Seminole's dark eyes peering in.

"Easy, kid." The old wolf's warning whisper just reached Jess. "I've tried to git here before . . . but it's been a heap too populous to be safe. Now, we gotta talk fast. I ain't so gymnastical as I usta be, an' I hate to think what'd happen, if ol' Napoleon here took a sudden scare."

Seminole was standing on his horse's back. That accounted for his being up here in the air.

Jess glanced behind. All was quiet. Faint and regular, he heard the snores of his guard. He leaned toward Seminole, whispering tensely: "Where's Ford?"

"Home," was the blessed answer. "An' he's doin' fine. He sent me here to. . . ."

But, eager as Jess was to know why Ford had sent him, he could not wait to take one big kink out of the threads.

"Did Spike take him home?" was the next question.

His heart leaped to the old man's cautious snort. "Spike? No. What put that in your head? Me an' Bart done it. We smelled trouble on the air that night, an' follered the scent upriver, comin' on a fresh trail goin' up to your place. We moseyed up there . . . mighty careful, for we knowed something was up. We found Ford in your cabin, an' yanked him out . . . two jumps ahead of the posse. He says you ain't to worry, kid. Says to tell you that when your trial comes up, he'll see you're cleared."

Old Seminole was all but unbalanced by the boy's frantic whisper: "I can't wait trial. You've got to get me out of here."

For, flashingly, with positive knowledge that Spike had

not taken Ford away, had not gone up to his cabin for that reason, the tangle unsnarled. Jess saw the perfect way to pay back Jim Fergus. A way that would settle every score — even the blood score. But he had to be out to do it. He must be free.

"You've got to get me out of here," he pleaded, his eyes sparks in the night. "Tell Ford I know who the other rustlers are . . . who put the Ten Wheel cows in my corral. But I've got to get out to prove it." Over and over, he iterated that, against Seminole's natural objections that jails were built to keep folks in, and that he would only be jumping out of the frying pan into the fire.

"Kid, they'll sure say you're guilty, if you run," insisted Seminole.

But as Ford had told Jess on that September day when he had mended his old saddle with high hopes, so Jess now told Seminole: "I can't be guiltier than they say I am."

His entreaties at last won the reluctant promise: "Waal, I'll tell Ford, an' see what he thinks." Then, with a fervent — "So long, kid! An' good luck." — Seminole dropped from sight.

The boy went back to his cot, his heart and soul on fire with thought. He would get out and prove it. He would put Fergus through the torture he had been through, smear him with the same black mud. Make him come whining on his knees to a Trailor.

Often as the reproachful face of the loyal, kind-hearted girl drifted between him and his vengeful plans, Jess crushed it down. He crushed it down with rushing thoughts of Ute Trailor. His father had been loyal, too, and always kind, but they had killed him. Maybe he deserved death in a way, but not that way — not like they had killed him. They were so strong for law, but they hadn't killed him lawfully. The state didn't kill for cows. Murdered him — that's what they'd done. And Dan — just a kid, just twenty-one — they had murdered Dan.

So for days he thought, and, crazy from such thinking, paced his narrow cell and panted to get out. He longed to get out and do what he had told Jetta no man could do, at least, not he, a Trailor — fight alone the whole Big Smoky range.

Would Ford aid him? Or would Ford insist on his standing trial, then come out at the sacrifice of self to prove Jess's innocence? He was capable of it. Jess had seen deep into the old man's soul that night. But he prayed Ford would not do so, and that he would find some way to free him before the trial.

Long, long days he waited, his Trailor eyes blue fire — thinking, thinking, with the mysterious stranger looming largely in his thoughts. Long, long nights he listened to a torment of suspense, slept not, lest he miss the prayed-for tap.

X
"A WHITE MAN"

It was two o'clock in the morning. Even the night owls in Salitas had gone to roost. The Ranger's Rest was dark, as befitted a respectable hostelry, catering to the best class of trade, but an alley view would have revealed a light still burning in a ground-floor room. Through the unshaded window, the stranger might have been seen, sitting in a rocker by the bed, his iron-gray head bowed on his chest, his steel-gray eyes fixed on the carpet at his feet. Dog-tired

171

as he was, his mind ran on and on, and would not let him rest.

He had been in the saddle from dawn till dark, visiting many ranches, and talking to the proprietor of each one. Each of these men had told him one thing, proving it to his reason, but his instinct told him they were wrong. He feared that the trouble lay within himself, feared that he was slipping, losing his grip. A fearful thought for a man of sixty to hold at 2 a.m.

Always he had believed in first impressions, had prided himself on his ability to make snap judgment of a man. Now he had his first failure to admit. The boy had fooled him. He would have sworn the kid was straight, that he was a victim of prejudice — natural enough under the circumstances, but cruel to the victim. He had felt that prejudice in the cold, heartless silence that reigned while the boy sat the red killer in the chute. He had seen it operate in the abominably cold-blooded way they froze him out after his plucky ride.

He had never taken such a fancy to anyone before. Why, he would have staked his honor on Jess Trailor. He nearly had. His professional honor, at least. He shuddered yet at the narrowness of his escape. He could thank the boy for it. Jess had refused his offer. Did not that prove that the kid had some shred of conscience left? There he went — snatching at straws to vindicate himself. He had been in the posse that had caught the boy red-handed with rustled stock.

Well — the gray stranger sighed — like father, like son, as the old saw went. The kid was Ute Trailor's son. What else could you expect? For one thing, he quickly replied to himself, he would have expected better work. Those doctored brands — clumsy stuff. He would have sworn that if the kid were a rustler, he would have been a clever one. And, deeply, the stranger sighed again.

There had been no more rustling since the arrest. With their leader caught, the Trailor gang must have taken fright and fled. It looked as though he would wind up his work here soon. He would sure be glad to get away. The boy haunted him, and had haunted him, since that day he had overtaken him on the road outside the Stampede grounds. There had been a look in his eyes when he turned down that job — a hungry, beaten, hopeless look — such as a man going to his execution might cast back on life. But even that look was not as haunting as the way he had looked up there, that night when they clamped the irons on. . . .

The stranger leaped to his feet, and snatched at the blue-nosed gun in his holster, as hands without flung wide his window sash. Then he stood there, helpless to use it, and, of a sudden, cold — not with the raw October wind sweeping in but with recognition of the face gazing through the window — the face that had haunted him.

A face aged five years in the three weeks since he had seen it. A face white with strange pallor, strained, with awful strain, and eyes imploring with an intensity that gave them a glow scarcely human. Eyes more like those of an animal, hard-pressed, yet fearing the sanctuary it must seek. The face of the jailed boy — Jess.

"You . . . ," the man gasped, as the boy stepped quickly over the sill, pulled down the shade, and came toward him, panting, wild-looking. "What does this mean? How did you get out?"

"I broke out!" cried Jess in a muffled, sobbing breath, his hands trembling on the stranger's arm. "I came straight to you for help."

"To me," the man groaned. "To me . . . of all men. You

173

know I've got to take you back."

The boy's blazing eyes held his unwaveringly. "But I'm sure you won't, Thorne."

Steeling himself to do it, yet afraid he would not, as he reacted to his first singular liking for this youth, the man whispered harshly: "Why not?"

"Because you ain't like them . . . you're white."

"You're guilty." Although too low to disturb the lightest sleeper in that house, Jack Thorne's tone was filled with reproach so bitter that it brought a hot film to the boy's eyes. "Guilty as sin . . . or you wouldn't run. An', boy, I believed in you."

"They framed me," Jess said fiercely. "An' I can prove it, Thorne. That's why I broke out . . . I couldn't work in there. You've got to believe in me again. You've got to give me that job. I couldn't take it then . . . but I've come to take it now."

That job. Speechless, Thorne stared at him. Was he in earnest? Yes — he saw — in deadly earnest.

"Do you know what you ask? You ask me to make you a special deputy for the Cattle Association. You . . . a rustler . . . a jail-breaker. Do you take me for a fool . . . or what?"

"A white man . . . I told you," flashed Jess. Then, as he gripped both Thorne's arms, as if by main strength to hold him to his promise, his story burst from him in a flood of hot, wild, broken words.

He took the stranger back to the cabin — back to the time when he and Dan had played there like any boys, whooping it up till the very rocks rang. He told of the barrier that had come between his folks and him, so that he could not get near them, could not even be pals with Dan. He told of the tragedies later that taught him the Trailor way did not pay, of that hard, hungry year in which he had

174

learned that a Trailor could not live honestly in Big Smoky range. Jess even told of Jetta — for Thorne was the kind of man you could tell — of the big part the girl had unconsciously played in his life. But not one word did he tell of Ford Cruze to this famed detective of the range. All else — though. . . .

Jess took the listener through all he had been through, showing no pity for himself, only the hard, brutal facts of a boy's struggle against fearful odds, bringing to Jack Thorne's eyes the first tears in years. He told how he had decided to stake his fate on the outcome of the Stampede — no need to tell the outcome to this man who had seen. He had vowed to "go Trailor" so he could not take that job. He would have been a rustler only for things that had come up. But he had not stolen those Seven Star cows — honest he had not. He explained how he had been lured from his cabin by the treacherous message, and had returned to find cows stolen from Jim Fergus in his corral.

"But I didn't put them there," he insisted passionately. "They done that . . . to put the blame on me. I know who. Let me catch them. Let me clean up the rustlin'. If you don't, Thorne, they'll send me up. An', after things quiet down, the stealin' will go on."

His eyes dropped before Thorne's query: "Who do you suspect?"

Jess could not tell him that. "Not even to you, I can't!" he exclaimed. "You've got to trust me. Let me work alone. Give me that job."

"Boy, you make it hard for me." Jack Thorne looked more than sixty then. "I can't do it . . . no, not if every word you say is true."

"Then" — and Thorne never forgot the look that accompanied that bitter speech — "you ain't the man I thought

175

you. You ain't no better than the rest."

"I'll see that you get a fair trial, Jess. If you can prove your story, you stand a good chance of acquittal."

"Yeah." Jess shrugged, defeated. "A fat chance. You know the size of any chance Big Smoky gives me. You've heard the talk."

Thorne knew — none better. It was all he had heard for weeks. He heard Jess now, in one last, frantic plea: "A chance from you . . . that's all I ask. If I find it's a blind trail . . . if I fall down . . . I'll give myself up to you. I swear."

Instinct told Thorne to do it, told him that the boy was no rustler. His job was to rid the range of rustlers. It was for that he had been sent in answer to Big Smoky's plea — not to convict Jess Trailor. Instinct told him that the task he had thought about wound up was not actually begun, that the boy could be of infinite aid to him.

"But how could you work? Every man in this country will be on your trail. They're bound to capture you."

"I'll take that chance."

Long and hard the association man looked at Jess, who was trembling with reborn hope. Then he said aloud, but to himself: "I am a fool . . . that kind of a fool."

Joy transfigured the weary youth. "You will. . . ."

"I will. But" — Thorne's hands fell heavily on Jess's shoulders — "boy, you listen to me . . . hard. I've got a clean record. I've worked hard for it. I'm proud of it. I've brought more cattle thieves to justice than any man in the state. Now . . . I'm blotching that record, aiding and abetting a fugitive from justice, empowering a suspected rustler to act for me, putting all I am, and hope to be, in your hands. Boy, my last blue chip is staked on you."

"You won't be sorry," promised Jess with bursting heart.

Their hands met in a long grip, then clutched in mutual

fear and guilt, as a yell from up the street, in the direction of the jail, the furious *clip-clop* of a running horse, routed the hush of night. But it was only a roistering 'puncher passing through Salitas.

Five minutes later the lights went out in the ground-floor room. The shade went up, and a dark figure stepped out, and slipped down the alley. The tenant of that room put down the sash, and dropped into his chair again, drugged with thought.

When, at last, he rose to look out, the stars were dying, the gray dawn was breaking, and Jess Trailor — armed with badge and written authority to take any law-breaker — was miles on his way up to the timbered notch where the Little Jack Pine flowed.

Early that morning news of the jailbreak flashed through town and rangeland. All morning curious crowds thronged the jail to see the sawed bars of the little window through which Jess Trailor, with outside aid, had managed his escape. Unanimously Big Smoky cursed its tolerance now. As the manhunt spread range-wide, swelling like the ripples on a troubled lake, they swore that they would not repeat the same mistake.

XI
" 'I'LL DO IT FOR YOU!' "

Up at Ford's place again. With the morning sun smiling, with all the jack pines laughing until every needle shook, with the mountain air crisp, perfumed with pine, heady as wine, air to make blood race and tingle, to blow prison fog from a cloudy mind, with a wilderness behind, and Jess Trailor free — free to range it, knowing it would hide and nourish those who knew and loved it.

With the two gaunt old wolves, Bart and Seminole, still grinning at how they had freed a young cub from the cage — leaving to watch the trails to Ford's place, to watch, as only wolves can watch, the prairies far below. With the fastest horse in Ford's band — which is to say, the fastest in all the range — saddled, waiting, to run with him at the first alarm.

Jess was feeling like a new man, refreshed, clean, in the best clothes Ford could "scare up" — the best he had worn in many a moon. He was feeling almost happy again, with Ford across the table from him — a little less bulky than before, with a few more touches of frost in his hair, and his cinnamon face shades lighter for the pain he had undergone. But well and strong.

Oh, it seemed good to Jess to be up at Ford's place again.

Solicitous as a mother cat with one kitten, Ford shoved the pan of biscuits at him.

"Quit nibblin', son, an' wade in. I outdone myself on them biscuits. An' that venison steak . . . dropped that buck myself, yesterday, on Huckleberry Ridge . . . a young 'un an' sure prime. An' have some more of this wild honey. Bart brung it in . . . 'lowed it would take the taste of jail chuck outta your mouth."

"It's sure some feed," Jess praised the meal, although he barely tasted it, his real hunger having been appeased by all this coddling.

"Waal, clean it up . . . then we'll talk."

But Jess could not get another bite down. He had to tell Ford all he knew, and was going to do — all about Jack Thorne. He did not know how Ford would take that. Pushing back his plate, he leaned on the table, earnestly studying his friend, at a loss how to begin.

But Ford broke the ice: "Seminole says you know who the other rustlers are, said you wanted to be out to get the goods on them an' clear yourself. Jess, I don't savvy that. But I hope you're right. An' if you be" — red tinged his features, and a flame flared in his eyes — "I'll handle 'em for you. Damn 'em, they plumb ruined me. I ain't got a cent left, an' my men's quit me . . . gone to greener fields. Bart an' Seminole's leavin' . . . with my blessin'. They'd had it in their heads for a long time to go on a prospect up in the Cassiar. So they're goin'. But me? I don't know what I'm a-goin' to . . . son, who are the rustlers?"

"Spike Travis an' Met Fergus!" cried Jess, his face hard. As he saw Ford's keen disappointment, he added: "They're the men who framed me. The men who shot you. The men who stole your herds."

"A wild guess," Ford said shortly. "Why, Spike's my man. I was his outlet for rustled stock. An' most of that stock came from the Seven Star . . . which lets Met out. Met wouldn't be apt to steal his own cows."

"His dad's cows," coolly corrected Jess. "An' they'd look like any man's to Met. I tell you he's low-down enough for that. He was with them that night . . . I saw him, two minutes after you was shot. Nobody else was near . . . unless Spike was. So it had to be one or the other of them done that. If Met was straight, he'd have taken them cows back home, or said something about seein' 'em before they was in my corral. He'd have made some report of shootin' a rustler. But he never opened his head about it at my hearing, or since. Why? Because he's a rustler, that's what he is. Ford, can't you see?"

"I see you're runnin' wild."

"All right." Jess leaned closer. "You heard Spike come to

179

the cabin for me, heard what he said. Well, Jetta never sent for me . . . she told me so herself. That ain't half. She told me Met rushed home about nine . . . which would be right after I seen him up there . . . an' got up a posse. Did he take it to look for a wounded rustler? No! He took that posse to my cabin. He knew Spike had driven the cattle there."

Ford Cruze jerked up in his chair. Behind his eyes, pure granite now, a storm was brewing. It grew as Jess continued: "Met must have seen them brands . . . known they was Seven Star cows. But he didn't care. Why not? Because he was in with Spike, sellin' his dad's cows to you, an' gettin' his share. But things was gettin' hot, an' they wanted to drag a red herrin' across their trail. I was the fish they picked. Met always had it in for me. So had Spike. After Spike sold them cows to you, they tried to get 'em back to plant on me an' have me blamed for all the stealin'. They didn't figure you'd put up a fight. But you did, an' they shot you. They'd about cleaned you out anyhow, an' Spike was through with you. It would have worked like a charm, if I hadn't gone in with you, been there that night, an' seen Met."

Ford saw it all — all Spike's treachery to himself, and the plot against Jess. Only the obviousness of the truth had kept him from seeing it long before this.

"That's where your herds went, Ford. They got your ten bucks a head for them cows, stole 'em back out of your hidin' place, an' resold 'em to someone outside the range. Made ten a head by passin' 'em through your hands, an' had you to tie the blame to if they got caught. They made double money on every cow they stole. Met's money mad. An' because he is money mad, I can get the goods on 'em both . . . with your help."

"Spike's skinned out." Ford's face was like a thundercloud. "I sent for him, wantin' to quiz him some myself. They said he'd gone. Mebbe he's gone for good. Mebbe he's just layin' low. It's a cinch he won't show up while you're loose. An' it's another cinch that I'll run down that coyote an' drag him from his hole."

But Jess was not concerned with Spike Travis. Old hate blazed in Trailor's eyes as he leaped to his feet. "Let Spike go, Ford. It's Met Fergus I want. An' I want to hit Jim Fergus through him. Fergus is loco over that no-good son. He don't know, won't believe, that Met's nothing but a tinhorn gambler, cheat . . . rotten spoiled. Fergus is afraid of me, has been since I was a kid. Afraid Met would take up with me. He'd as soon have Met exposed to smallpox as to a Trailor. All my life he's sicked Met on me, an' backed him up. I'm scum, he said. Well, he forgot . . . scum's on top. I'm goin' to balance accounts with Fergus. You'll help me, Ford?"

The old man gritted: "I'll skin him alive."

"Met's got plenty of money now," Jess went on more quietly, "thanks to their crooked dealin's with you. They've laid off rustlin', so folks'll sure think they had the right man when they had me. But when he needs more, he'll hunt up Spike. It's your job to see he needs it, *pronto!*"

"Hijack him?" The old rogue was more than willing.

"No, I got a better way doped out. Once he's broke, he'll hunt up Spike, an' they'll go on the rustle again. An' when they do, we'll be there and we'll fix. . . ."

"It's taps for Spike Travis?" grimly Ford vowed.

Slowly Jess came toward him around the table, his eyes uneasy. "Ford, we ain't goin' at it that way. We're goin' at it legal. I'm goin' to arrest Met Fergus, convict him in open court, an' put him behind the bars."

"Arrest him?" affectionately Ford ridiculed the boy.

181

"You . . . a hunted man yourself. An' believe me, there'll be a hunt. Why, you talk like you was a regular range dick, son."

"I am," said Jess with a nervous tremor, glad to have broken the news at last. "I'm workin' with the association man Big Smoky sent for. I've got authority to arrest any rustler."

As Ford still smiled tolerantly, Jess threw back his coat, displaying his badge, drew out the paper, and, clearing a place on the table, spread it out before his friend. His heart sank as the old rustler recoiled from it, from *him*, as from contamination. No affection was in his shocked cry as he rose, gripping the table: "An' you . . . a Trailor! Ute's boy! An' I loved you like a son. I . . . I'd 'a' died for you!"

Cut to the quick by his wrathful pathos, trying to make Ford understand, Jess earnestly explained how he had met Jack Thorne. How Thorne had believed in him, and wanted his help then, but he couldn't give it because. . . .

"I'd promised to come to you, Ford, if I lost. But when I broke out last night, I went to him, an' he still believed in me. He gave me this chance to clear myself . . . square myself . . . an' he's goin' to help me. But I . . . I can't work without you."

"A lot of help you'll get from me," Ford said coldly. He turned his back on Jess, and walked to the door with slow and heavy tread.

"Don't throw me down!" Jess followed, pleading. "Now, when I need you. It's my big chance . . . the only one I've ever had. I won't have another. Ford, you know how I'm looked on here. Oh, I could go away where folks don't care who I am, but neither do I care about them. It's home folks I care about. I've got to fight my way up here. An' even if I could do it alone, I wouldn't go up without you. You mean too much. I won't leave you behind."

The old man was touched. He dared not look at Jess. A range detective! Like all his kind, he felt for them a deep aversion, an instinctive loathing. The boy was one — and wanted, needed his help. Heaven only knew how much Ford deep down in his heart wanted to help.

"You won't be turnin' traitor," Jess insisted. "Your men's gone. Your band's broke up. There's just Spike . . . Spike who shot an' left you . . . never come back to see was you dead. Or he knew Met shot you . . . and left you just the same. Think what you owe Spike."

"I don't pay my debts that way!" The retort was gruff.

Jess gave up. His dark face gleamed with a reckless light. He went back to the table and picked up badge and paper. "Then these go in the fire!" he exclaimed. "An' I go back to jail. I thought you meant what you said that night . . . thought I meant something to you."

This was too much for Ford. "Boy," he groaned, coming back, "you sure do."

"Then go straight along with me. You ain't quittin' winner. You lost more than you ever won. You're gettin' old, Ford. Look ahead. What is there? Nothing! This will be a new game. Better starve, you said, than lay in some hole an' feel life go out in the dark. Better starve, I say, than lay in the kind of hole I been in, an' die by inches."

The old man staggered to his chair and fell into it. "I . . . I can't, Jess. I told you . . . my feet's in the mud."

"Then pull 'em out . . . by helpin' me clean up the rustlers. Wipe off the mud."

Ford's eyes closed. All his life he had been a crook. Circumstances, or some quirk in an otherwise normal brain, had warped his moral vision. But like most men of his type, he had his moments of deep yearning for self-respect and the respect of his fellow man. A strange, rapt expression dawned on his face.

"Ford Cruze . . . a range dick," he muttered plaintively to himself. "Sell myself for. . . ." He looked up to see the earnest tears in Jess Trailor's eyes, and the love shining through.

"Son," he reached up his hand, "I'll do it for you."

And so the new game was begun at once.

While it was in progress, the last of Ford's men quietly and eternally faded from Big Smoky range. For Bart and Seminole, starting north on their long-planned trip, into the land where wolves were wolves, went so far that no word of them ever came back. Spike Travis remained in hiding, his absence of too little interest to the public at large to be even noted.

The hunt for Jess Trailor went on. Goaded by Jim Fergus, Sheriff Carey did his level, futile best to retake the fugitive, persisted long after the first frenzy passed, and the range fell back into its old routine, solaced by the conviction that the last Trailor had been run out of the country.

The black-eyed girl at the Seven Star prayed that he had, but feared he had not. Feared it not for his own sake, but for those she loved. Often her eyes would lift to the wild, blue heights, and her heart told her he was there, as it told her that he was responsible for this gloom hanging over the Seven Star — the foreshadowing of some blight about to fall.

There had been a morbid change in Met since that night he had led the posse to Jess. Some secret fear, remorse, was driving him to the devil by every short cut. He was in a state bordering on frenzy, almost a stranger in his home, merely flinging himself in and out, all fury and excitement. Jetta was beside herself with anxiety, and even Jim Fergus was troubled in his heart about the son he worshipped.

All this while, Jack Thorne, playing his part of watchful waiting, kept his ears open and his mouth shut. He seldom left his room at the Ranger's Rest after dusk had fallen, but from his window kept lone vigil, his eyes lifted to the hills — to one lone hill that stood out from the peaks behind, a bold rock dome — Old Baldy — rising like an island in a sea of green. Here, if success were his, the boy on whom Thorne's reputation was staked would light the signal fire that would bring aid to him and sure ruin on the Seven Star.

XII
" 'YOU'VE MET JESS TRAILOR AGAIN!' "

There was in Salitas, and but a stone's throw from the Ranger's Rest, a place called the Smoke House. It was a rude, barn-like, dim-lit place, where local ranch hands could pit their wages against their luck at cards. Needless to say, it was well frequented. Probably its most consistent frequenter was Met Fergus of the Seven Star.

Here, in the Smoke House, while barely out of short trousers, Met had learned to play. He had taken to poker like a duck to water, acquiring a passion for the game, if no particular skill, until he came at sorry last to seek it, not as a recreation, for the clash of wits, the game itself, as did most of the other boys, but greedily, avidly, as a narcotic addict seeks his drug. He came for the physical and mental relief of liberating the gambling fever that burned intolerably in his blood, came for the last few weeks, to seek it for the oblivion it brought.

But Met was finding it hard to get opponents. Hard-working waddies were bluffed out by the heavy bankroll he displayed, and balked at his surly temper, his abusiveness that robbed the game of pleasure. For, of late, too, his arrogance had passed all bounds.

But this night, some time after Jess Trailor's escape, he had bullied three men into playing with him. The heated session was right at its height when a man entered who had been for years a stranger to such haunts. He was a big, easy-going old fellow, with kind eyes and a genial smile, one who few of the Smoke House inmates recognized, but who was enthusiastically greeted by these. For no one could know and be anything but cordial to Ford Cruze.

Talking briefly with each in turn, Ford drifted casually from table to table, coming at last to the one where Met sat, wholly absorbed in the game.

Chuck Saunders, chancing to glance up and see him standing behind Met's chair, hailed his advent with great relief.

"Take my place," he invited, pushing his last chip in the pot. Rising, he added with a sardonic grin: "If you want to set in on a friendly game."

Ford nodded thanks, and quietly took the chair opposite Met. His eyes hardened at Met's violent start when he saw him, at the sickly gray that overspread his features. Met was afraid of him. Then, Jess was right. But playing his game with Jess, in which personal vengeance had no part, Ford smiled disarmingly at Met.

However, the guilty youth was not disarmed by it. Here was one man with whom he had no desire to play, from whom he wished only to get away. He growled, half rising: "I'm out . . . I'm sick of this piker game."

"Better stay," softly insinuated Ford, "a round or two, anyway."

Met sat down.

Cards went around. Ford saw the nervous temper with which Met took up his and the drops that broke out on his forehead, and, to give him a chance to get his guilty soul in hand, turned his attention on the other two players.

Dave Martin was dealing. He sat on Ford's left, looking mighty uncomfortable, as did the Fiddleback waddy on his right. Evidently Met had been making it hot for them. The old rustler chuckled inwardly. He had learned poker long before these kids were in swaddling clothes, and learned it very well, indeed. So it was not strange that almost from the first hand Met's luck changed.

Nor did Met think it strange. It would jinx anyone — playing with a dead man. Up there, on the riverbank that night, Ford had sure dropped like dead. He had lived for a month with thoughts of him dead, horrid thoughts up there in the brush, horrid nightmares, that woke him up, to hear, with unnerving horror, coyotes howling up there. . . .

Steadily he lost, and plunged more recklessly after his losses. A poor loser always, he cursed the cards dealt him, cursed the players, lost all restraint. Throwing a handful of bills on the table, he cried hoarsely: "I'm callin' a five-buck ante!" His bold eyes flickered with sullen fire. "Make it a real game."

"Then I cash in." The Fiddleback waddy quit. "You may be a millionaire, but I work for my money."

"Me, too," said Dave, getting up. "Met must mint that stuff. I don't see. . . ."

"What don't you see?" furiously Met cut in on him. "It's real stuff, ain't it? Don't you like the color of my money?"

"Oh, sure." Dave shrugged. "It's real enough. But I'd

sure like your formula for makin' it."

Met's jaw shot out, and he started up. "I'd like to know if it's any of your business how I. . . ."

"Steady, boys," put in Ford placatingly. "Come on, Met. I'll give you a run for your money."

So they played on alone. Steadily Ford won the confidence and cash of the Seven Star's son and heir. For Met, lulled into the belief that Ford could have no suspicion about that night, threw himself into the game with utter abandon, and lost, and lost. Well Ford knew how to handle Met's type of gambler. If he quit loser, he would be wild to play again and recoup his losses. If he won, these games would end. So Met found himself several hundred dollars in the hole when at a late hour the game broke up.

"Give me a show to win that back," was his insolent order. "I'll expect you here tomorrow night."

"I'll be here," Ford agreed.

That night, and every night, as Met left the Smoke House, a shadow materialized from somewhere and haunted his trail. He did not see it — he just felt it. Ride wild, as he did, the shadow still pursued, and he could not shake it. Was it conscience? No. It had substance and intelligence. It had memory — that shadow. Only when Met was in his room for the night — or the tag end left of the night — was he free from it. He only forgot it when deep in sleep, or deep in those fevered games with Ford.

For a week the games went on. Met's money was scientifically taken from him, also, his every asset that he could convert to cash, then every Seven Star account that he could collect without his father's knowledge. At last, in his frenzy to regain what he had lost, he began to give checks to repay his gambling scores, checks which Ford found to be worthless. When he held a staggering sum in worthless checks, Ford dropped his suavity.

"Cover these, *pronto!*" he demanded coldly. "Make 'em good, or I take 'em to your dad."

Met, rallying from the shock of his changed demeanor, his terror of the threat, had dared him to do it. "Go ahead," he blustered, "an' see where you land! I know a thing or two myself."

"All the knowledge in the universe" — Ford's words had meaning and an icy edge — "ain't in your head. Rustlin's one crime, an' attempted murder's something else. Cover these checks by Saturday, or you'll find yourself charged with both."

Leaving Met to digest that, Ford Cruze stepped outside for a word with a shadow. "Watch your step . . . he's about to blow up." Then he swiftly drew into the gloom, as Met rushed past and hurriedly flung himself onto his horse.

Back to the Seven Star pounded the ruined youth, at a pace to tax any horse on that range — except the fastest horse on Ford's place, which the shadow rode. But not to spend the tag end of this night at home, for he left the panting beast in the drive, flung into the house and out, leaped into the saddle again, and tore up the road. All so swiftly that Jetta, bursting out of the house with him, running down the path after him, distractedly crying — "Met! Met!" — came between him and his shadow, and staggered back, white hands fluttering to her throat in terror, lips moving in a husky whisper: "Jess!"

Jess had hidden his horse in the shrubbery, waiting until it was safe to follow Met. He was just emerging when she ran by him, and now stood in his tracks, powerless to speak or move as she came toward him.

"Why did you come here?" she breathed, glancing about as on that other midnight when she had met him on the road out there. "They'll catch you. They think you've gone."

He did not answer. He was too stunned. He had locked her out of his heart. Yet, here, tonight, with success in sight, his soul was stormed by the feeling that knows no locks. He had no tongue, although all the love he had renounced spoke eloquently from his burning eyes.

"Jess" — piteously she wrung her hands, "you mean harm to Met. He's doing wrong. You know it. You're after him."

Still he did not answer. In terror of what she had seen in Met's eyes tonight, of the pull that had hung for weeks over the Seven Star, she made a broken appeal to this boy's love for her — a plea for self, since she dared not appeal for Met.

"Jess, we've been friends always. Don't make me suffer. He's my brother. I can't help what Met does."

Jess could not help what his folks did. Long, long ago, she had said the same words of him. But he had suffered, was suffering now — torn to pieces by the terrible tug between his love and resolution. His folks had paid for what they had done. So must Met pay — like them.

"You said you'd do anything for me." She was abject in her desire to avert the tragedy she sensed "You said . . . you'd give me the lining of your heart to make me moccasins."

Speech broke from him then, in tone strained and unnatural. "You've got it, Jetta. But . . . it's been so walked on . . . it won't hold together."

For the first time in her life, she saw Jess Trailor's head hanging, and the pity of it tore her. But always she had been a loving sister, the stanch protectress of a weak, erring brother.

She said: "I'll fight you, Jess . . . for Met. You force me

to be your enemy." She, who had always been with him, was now against him. "I'll tell Dad I saw you here."

If she did that, all hope was over. He would go back to jail. But he knew what it was to agonize over a brother. Swinging up and putting spurs to his horse — knowing, with crowning pain, that he need not shut his heart on Jetta, that she had taken herself out of his life forever — he said sadly: "If you do, Jetta . . . I won't blame you."

Straight from him, with all her horror fresh upon her, Jetta Fergus went to seek her father. She found him sitting at his desk, staring at an open ledger, with death in his eyes.

"Dad," she said, with dreadful calm, "you can charge this up to your own account."

Startled by her presence, by her words, cryptic, accusing, he sprang up. "Girl, what do you mean?"

"I mean, Dad, you haven't kept your own doorstep clean. You've been too concerned with the Trailors. Now, what does the ledger show? Jess Trailor has grown up to be everything you hoped Met to be . . . a fine, strong, clean man. And Met is all you ever accused Jess of being . . . a sneak, a thief, a rustler."

Jim Fergus was on the verge of violent utterance when she checked him by her very indifference to any utterance of his.

"Oh, it's true," she stated, in that same helpless tone. "Met's been gambling heavily . . . you know that. Dora Saunders told me Chuck said he'd lost five hundred dollars at the Smoke House last night. Where did he get that sum to lose? He's lost hundreds more in the last week. He stole the diamond ring you gave me for graduation. Oh, he owned it, when I faced him. Here are a few more statistics . . . he's been thick with Spike Travis for a year. Spike and Met planted those cows on Jess. Met was with Spike that night. Spike disappeared when Jess escaped. He's afraid of Jess. Met's been afraid, too, you've seen it from. . . ." Even her high carriage wavered before her father's terrible gaze that went right through her. But she steeled herself for what remained: "Dad, Jess Trailor is out to settle accounts, and he'll have no more mercy on you now than you had on him."

Reaching out suddenly, he grasped her shoulders, bent her back, looked deeply into her big, frightened eyes, demanding: "You've seen him! He's on this range? You've met *Jess Trailor* again?"

Her lips parted, but no sound came. Losing his head in his blind dread of this thing coming on him, he shook her, hoarsely demanding at each shake: "Tell me! Tell me!"

XIII
" 'YOU AN' ME . . . IT CAN'T BE!' "

Away from the Seven Star, under the clasped hands of the skeleton willows, and up the highway, Jess tore after Met. He rode furiously, mile after mile, listening behind for sounds that would indicate that the desperate girl had put Jim Fergus on his trail, and listening ahead for sign that he was overtaking Met. Coming to where a dark wood road forked off, he hauled up, and found the fresh tracks of a racing horse plowing into it. Then, swerving his own horse, he dashed up it, climbing the black slopes where this road broke up into a hundred trails. He heard Met's horse ahead and slackened pace, the terrible tension on his nerves slackening.

Now let them ride for him. Nothing could stop that which was coming to pass. Met had to rustle that money —

rustle. Jim Fergus would know what it meant to have the rustler sign pinned on him. For there would be plenty to say he was in with Met, and that all his talk about losses was a blind to cover their thefts. It would hurt Fergus, too, in more ways than it had hurt him. For the bigger you are, the harder you fall. Jess had not been even a pebble on this beach, but Fergus was mighty as Standing Rock. His fall would shake the whole range.

So Jess thought, as hour after hour he stalked Met, following him up one ridge after another, twisting back on mountain spurs, climbing nearer the yellow stars, up in the wilds above Ford's place, up in the highest peaks of the Big Smoky range. He was assailed, at last, by the fear that he and Ford had overplayed their hand — had scared Met out of the country. For this trail was a short cut to Crestline, a railroad town on the other side of the divide.

What he would have done in that case, Jess did not know, and did not need to know. For Met suddenly sheered off the trail, striking north through a dark and narrow defile. Jess, pursuing him as closely as he might with safety, topped a rise overlooking a small valley, hidden away from the world in the heart of the mountains. His heart beat fast as he saw beyond the dark blob that was Met a host of dark blobs that were cattle. Cattle — up here. A big herd. And a cabin, so new that the chopped ends of the logs and barked spots gleamed white in the starlight. Someone must have built it for a retreat — a place to hold cattle.

Jess halted in the trees, as Met reined up at the cabin, waited until he had passed inside, and a light flared from the window. Then, careful to keep out of the view of the house, he rode among the cattle and studied the brands. Every one had been worked over, and, reading under the spurious brands, he identified cows from the Ace of Clubs,

S Bar Three, Fiddleback, and almost every other Big Smoky ranch. His blood ran like fire to see, thickly sprinkled among them, cows that had belonged to the Seven Star, but which now wore the familiar — for him, all but fatal — Ten Wheel brand.

All the stock was in poor shape, and he surmised that the marketable stuff had been sold and driven off, and that somebody was holding these here until they were in condition. A sudden suspicion as to who that somebody was made Jess wild to get to the cabin.

Making a wide detour, he came up on the timbered slopes behind it. Here he left his horse. Slipping down through the dense, low-spreading firs, whose matted needles made a sponge underneath that soaked up all sound, he reached the rear wall of the cabin. Here he crouched, listening to a voice within that confirmed his suspicion, a voice that whined protest at the demand made by Met. The voice of Spike Travis.

"Not a red cent! I've dug up all I'm a-goin' to."

Then Met's lordly tone, bullying him: "We'll see about that! I've got to cover them checks. . . ."

"That's your look-out," Spike squeaked like a rabbit nerved to put up a fight. "You done the dancin' . . . now pay the piper. I warned you not to gamble. Besides, you're borrowin' trouble. There ain't an *hombre* in Big Smoky got the nerve to take them checks to Jim Fergus."

"This *hombre* has" — Met seemed to enjoy telling him — "the *hombre* who's got 'em."

"Who's got 'em?"

"Ford Cruze."

Jess could envision Spike shrinking back. He heard Met's taunting laugh.

"Jolts you, huh, to know he's alive? Well, it did me

some. Jolted me into gamblin' with him when he blowed into the Smoke House that night. He sharped me till he got them checks, then threatened to show me up if I didn't make 'em good by Saturday."

"Why didn't you come back at him?" bleated Spike when he could. "You got his number. Just say the word rustler. Go back . . . bluff him."

Met jeered at that. "Don't you suppose I tried it? He don't bluff. Told me to go to it, an' he'd see I kept him company on that charge . . . also for them shots I took at him. He meant it, an' you'd better dig that money up."

"I ain't got it."

"Then help me git it. We'll pull another raid. . . ."

"You fool!" Fear of Ford nerved Spike. "That's what he wants . . . not your money. You got Ford Cruze on our trail. He's out to revenge young Trailor. You can do as you like, but as for me . . . I'm pullin' my freight, *pronto!*"

Jess heard a chair scrape back, and Met's voice, ugly, threatening: "No, you don't. You got me into this, an' you'll help me out. I warn you, I won't take the blame alone. We've got to buy Cruze off. An' since Peters won't buy any of this poor stuff till the smoke blows over, we've got to rustle a bunch that he will take.

"My old man's got a band of prime two-year-olds on the range above Hangman Creek . . . he's plannin' to ship 'em for the Thanksgivin' trade. Peters will take 'em like a shot, an' pay cash. We can drive 'em through to Crestline, an' have the money before they're missed."

"It ain't safe." Jess could tell by his voice that Spike was cowed.

"We've got to take some chance," Met had the grace to admit. "Though I can't see much at that. We'll sock the Ten Wheel Brand on 'em, an', if anything comes up, we'll do a fade away, an' they'll blame Jess Trailor."

By the long silence that followed Jess knew that Spike was thinking it over. Then Met went on: "They'll think Trailor's back again, an' they'll be too busy huntin' him to suspect anyone else. Listen. . . ."

Tensely Jess listened to every word, as they plotted their downfall. He and Ford could not have planned it better. When he had learned that the pair would stay here until the following night, he went back to his horse.

From a brushy point he watched the cabin through dark and dawn, all that next day, unconscious of time, of hunger, or thirst, conscious of nothing but pain. For lying there in the chill, damp leaves, with his trampled heart and burning eyes, Jess lived his whole life over again. He tortured himself by reliving his every moment with Jetta, was tortured by the thought that she had appealed to him, and he had failed her.

She thought he was after Met to clear himself and escape prison. She did not know that fate had placed the whole Fergus family in power, that he must use that power — not for himself, or Ford, or Jack Thorne, who depended on him, but for something bigger than any of them — to settle accounts for his own father and brother. She had given him the cue when she said: "I'll fight you, Jess . . . for Met." So must he be true to his own — and forget.

The long lane had turned — perhaps into life's highroad, at last. For failure tonight was not in the cards, stars, or wherever portent of failure lies. But the boy had no thrill of success. Raising himself from the cold earth, he looked far off in the direction of the Seven Star, his arms stretched out, and with a sobbing breath, sad as the November wind mourning in the firs over his head, he moaned: "You an' me . . . it can't be."

196

Sunset colored the sky, and at the sun's red sinking, the two men left the cabin and rode down the valley. Jess, following them, came again under the yellow stars into Big Smoky range. He followed them as far as Old Baldy, then let them go their calamitous way alone.

Ascending the twining trail to begin payment of his long-standing account, the boy was engulfed by such loneliness as he had never known.

"I'll square you, Dad," broke his strangled cry on the night. "I'll square you, Dan."

He would square them — and then? His eyes burned into the future, and he saw — nothing. An icy coldness howled from the heights above him. A shooting star gleamed across the heavens, and dropped with a shower of cosmic sparks into the little cañon so long the home of the Trailors.

That night, looking out of his window, Jack Thorne saw a fire blaze high on Old Baldy. Joy sprang into his eyes. As he snapped on his guns, speedily preparing for a hard night ride, he muttered with tremulous joy: "There's nothing wrong with me. I can pick a winner yet. Heaven bless him . . . that fire-eyed lad."

XIV
" 'I'M WITH YOU, JESS!' "

"I need your help to make a capture." That much Jack Thorne told Sheriff Carey, when he picked him up at the jail. That much he told ranchers who he hastily mustered from the ranches passed — and no more. Not even to the Seven Star rancher, when they pulled up there, although, strangely enough, Fergus asked nothing, then, or as they galloped along. He seemed to have a clamp on his tongue, acted like a man in mortal terror that somebody would tell him something. Or so thought Ford Cruze, who had not needed to be told even that much. For Ford had stayed on in Salitas to watch for the signal fire on Baldy. Seeing it, he figuratively threw up his hat with three silent, heartfelt cheers for Jess, and was ready, waiting on Blaze, to join the posse unobtrusively as it dashed out of town.

Swiftly this posse pursued the same route as the other had taken that night when Jess was their quarry. Most of the galloping men believed they were riding for Jess Trailor again. Thoughts of him were in every mind, save that of Jack Thorne. For, as they neared Standing Rock, from whose shadow the boy had watched the first posse pass, Thorne took worried note of one of his riders. A half-grown kid, not more than sixteen, but packing a gun as big as himself. Where on earth had they picked him up? There was man's work afoot — no place for a kid. Already he looked scared sick.

Thorne was on the verge of ordering the kid back, when he saw a rider emerge from the gloom of the road, a rider who waited for them — Jess Trailor. Thorne had expected to meet the boy somewhere along here. He was calling a halt, to prepare these men for Jess, who was to them still a criminal, a fugitive, when a muffled scream startled him. He turned to see the kid staring past him in horror, and saw Ford Cruze — who had been watching like a hawk for some such move — strike down the gun Jim Fergus had drawn on the waiting rider.

"None of that!" shouted the range detective, spurring between the posse and Jess. "Sheriff, he's workin' for me.

I've known his whereabouts all this time. It's him who called you out for this ride."

Amazed, but plainly distrustful, they ringed about Jess. His dark face, shaded by his sombrero, was immobile, unreadable. But his eyes gleamed on Jim Fergus. Something in them removed the clamp on the rancher's tongue, put him in a frenzy.

"You see him, Carey!" he shouted at the sheriff. "He's back . . . that rustler . . . that jail-breaker! Back . . . facin' you, bold as brass. I demand his immediate arrest!"

Uncertainly the sheriff looked from Fergus to Thorne. "Trailor . . . ," he began.

Coldly Thorne cut in: "Let him alone till this night's work is over. Then if you want him, I'll produce him. Carey, you know my reputation. I'll be responsible for him."

Jack Thorne's word was warrant enough for the sheriff of Salitas County. But Jim Fergus turned on him furiously: "Ain't you takin' a lot of responsibility on yourself!"

"If I am," Thorne said imperturbably, "I'm equal to it." Then, addressing the boy who had promised him he would not be sorry and had kept that promise: "Well, Jess?"

"I've located the men you want," Jess reported to Thorne alone. "They're up here now . . . workin' over brands on some young Seven Star steers. I'll take you up . . . an', when you've caught 'em, I'll show you their cattle cache."

Stunned by this strange turn of events, Big Smoky ranchers followed a Trailor, expectant somehow of the unusual and, somehow, fearful. They ascended the dark, winding ridges to Hangman Creek in silence, save for the creak and clank of riding gear.

On the way, Jess spoke but once. That was when, almost

at the ledge from where he had promised them a view of the rustlers in operation, he noticed that Jim Fergus was lagging. An odd circumstance, when cow thieves were abroad, and his own cows being stolen.

"How come?" he demanded, his eyes burning on the man he suspected of killing his father. "I thought this sort of thing was right in your line. Get up here in the front row. Somebody might get in a bullet ahead of you."

He never forgot the look he got — not a look of hate, and the first he had ever had from this man that was not hatred. But such a look of fear, despair, of all hope done, as he had once seen in the eyes of a dying buck.

On the top of the ledge, Jess halted the men and, warning them against making a sound, led them on foot to the rocky point from where they could see, in the swale below, a small fire burning. And about it two men. Who? From that height there was no telling, and the flickering shadows of the fire distorted their figures, but there was no doubting their activity. For, as the posse watched with rising anger, one of the men threw a steer and held him, while the other drew a glowing iron out of the fire, and, stooping, ran a brand on the bellowing animal. Then they released it and drove it back, roped another, and threw it.

"Reckon we've seen enough." Thorne's mutter was grim. So was his order, when the vengeful men were on their horses: "Now for it. Quiet as you can . . . but fast."

At breakneck speed they tore down the slope, Jess forcing his horse close to that of Jim Fergus and pounding with him through tearing brush, down in an avalanche of rolling stone. Startled, the rustlers looked up, saw the riders coming, and, abandoning iron and steer, plunged for their horses. Thorne's arm went up. His gun spoke twice. The smaller figure halted, reeled, then pitched on his face and lay without a quiver. The other, leaping over him as he ran through a hail of bullets, made a flying mount and vanished. But not from the sight of Jess, who broke from the rest and spurred after, followed by only one rider, the kid, whom Thorne had all but sent back.

The rest, wild to know who was guilty of the rustling if Jess Trailor was not, rushed on down to the fallen man. They were surprised — but asked themselves why they should be — when they turned his face to the fire, and identified the Seven Star man, Spike Travis.

"He ain't dead yet," said Ford, who had turned him over, "but near it."

Spike knew it, as for the last time he opened his eyes on life, and these faces bent over him, focusing on the face of the man he had wronged.

"Boss," he gasped, death's throttling grip on him already "a word . . . alone. . . ."

Respecting death, wherever they met it, the men drew back. Fergus knelt by him.

"Boss" — awful was that rattling gasp, that swimming gaze — "must tell . . . name . . . my partner. . . ."

Awful was the cry of Jim Fergus: "In heaven's name, don't speak it."

The rustler, so soon to be in eternity, had pity. Qualities he had lacked in life came to Spike dying. The coyote look had left his face. It was filled with remorse. "I . . . won't. I'm sorry. We been at it eight months. Till the last two . . . we passed the cows to . . . another man. . . ."

"Who?"

Spike's humid eyes rolled toward the men watching. Death had foreshortened his gaze, but it reached Ford Cruze. Ford, who had heard every word steeled himself for the next, knowing it would pull him back in the mire, would tear him from the boy, who tonight was blazing his way to the highroad of life, knowing, now, how desperately, how honestly he longed to go with him.

"Boss . . . I won't . . . name him, either. I done him . . . dirt . . . aplenty. . . ." Thus, fully, Spike atoned for his treachery. "I . . . I'm . . . kickin' out . . . call Carey. . . ."

In terror of what he might confess to the sheriff, but unable to refuse a dying man's last request, Fergus signaled the sheriff.

"What is it, Spike?" Carey asked gently, dropping on one knee at his side.

Spike came far back to say it: "I . . . framed . . . Jess Trailor. Straight kid . . . I put them . . . Ten Wheel cows . . . in his corral."

"Uhn-huh. Why did you do it?"

"Old grudge. Ute gypped me . . . hated his breed. . . ." Spike made a tremendous effort to finish. "I squealed on him . . . to Fergus. Guided the posse . . . there. My shot got . . . Ute. Fergus . . . give . . . job . . . Seven Star. . . ."

His lids fell beneath an immovable weight. The flaring sage fire showed death in his face.

"Spike," Carey shook him, "who helped you tonight?"

With a wild and inarticulate cry, Jim Fergus thrust himself before Spike, as though bodily to hold back that reply. But there was no need.

Spike had died.

A mountain mile away, Jess Trailor was hard on the heels of the other rustler. They had Spike, and he would get Met. Fast as was the horse Met cruelly spurred in his terror, it was no match for the fastest horse on Ford's place. Steadily he gained on Met. Doggedly another rider hung close behind. Hearing, Jess wished with all his soul that it was Jim Fergus. He wanted Fergus there when he ran Met to earth. But glancing back, under the interlacing pines that dimmed the moonlight, he saw that it was too small a man to be the Seven Star rancher, or Ford. Beyond that he did not care, did not give a second glance, for he could not spare a glance from Met. And lucky for him that he did not.

For, seeing his pursuer was gaining, Met swung, and a gun glinted up in his hand. Jess ducked at the flash, but the bullet lifted his hat. He returned the fire with unerring aim, knocking Met's gun from his hand, and was ready, when Met leaped down and ran for it. Down himself, Jess was after him in a bound, bidding him stop, or he would shoot, in that commanding tone Met had heard once and obeyed — choking back his insults on that day of the Stampede. Hearing, now, he turned — no longer a bully, but a trembling, cowering hulk of a man — to meet certain exposure and ruin.

Jess, advancing with ready gun, heard the other rider plunge up and dismount, but he did not heed him. He wanted no help in the reckoning — for at last the reckoning had come. He was about to pay back Jim Fergus and Met, wipe out every insult he had taken from them, wipe out the blood score. . . .

Suddenly the boy stiffened. Despair seized him, bitter as death. For, as the other rider stepped up behind him, he felt the cold muzzle of a gun press into his back. It was no use. Innocent or not — Big Smoky would not work with a Trailor. In that despair, Jess made his choice. Big Smoky could finish him, but he would get Met first. Met could not get away with this. His nerves tensed. . . .

"Run, Met!" frantically screamed the voice behind Jess.

Faintness came on him, his whole body trembled. For it was Jetta. Jetta who had ridden with him. Jetta holding the weapon, trembling herself, for he felt the gun tremble.

"Run, Met . . . run!" in rising hysteria she begged her brother, who dared to run, facing that gun in the hand of Jess Trailor. There was in her cry all the sharp agony with which Jess had cried — "Dan! Dan!" — on that rainy night at the siding, bringing vividly home to him the enormity of what he had done. He had brought that on Jetta, all that shame — that untold pain. On Jetta, who would feel it most — more than her father. Jetta, who had stood up for him when nobody else had, who was already breaking with it, for he felt that gun shaking.

Jess knew he could not go through with it. Hate of the Ferguses, father and son, could not stand before his mad, desperate love for the sister and daughter. Met was free as air to go, as far as he was concerned.

"Jetta, I. . . ." He was turning to tell her so, when, with a roar like all the multiplied sounds of earth, the gun exploded.

He drew up slowly, a piteous look of amazement stamping itself on his face, and on the heart of the girl forever. Then he fell. Over his body brother and sister stared at each other.

"Good girl," said Met huskily, free as air to go, as far as Jess Trailor was concerned, but never, never, to be free of the awful horror in his sister's face then. She heard neither his praise nor his swift fleeing — for, judging others by himself, Met judged that Spike would have squealed on him if he lived — and he stood not upon the order of his going.

He left the dazed, crazed girl there in the desolate night woods, alone with her lover, shot down because of him. For Jetta had loved Jess since the days when she had smuggled candy, apples, and cake to school for him, and he did her examples. Always, at home or abroad, she had taken his part. She had loved him all the years of their separation, and that love had flowered into something beautiful, deathless, now that she was a woman. Courted, she was, by half the boys in Big Smoky. But to them she was all moods and whims, entirely heartless. To Jess, she was all heart. Pride prevented his taking a step toward her. Having no pride — only love — where he was concerned, she went toward him. She would have gone all the way, but now that. . . .

Now she swayed, and crumpled slowly to her knees beside him. Her black eyes were dreadfully wide, but mercifully not comprehending. Her sombrero had fallen, and her short, black hair hung about her face — the face of a tragic and broken woman. She lifted his dark head to her breast, and, when it kept falling back, she reproved him: "Jess, keep your head up."

When he did not, she was afraid they had beaten him, and she piteously pleaded: "I'll help you. It's you and me against the rest of them. Hold out a little longer, Jess. Something will turn up. Just a little longer . . . for my sake, Jess!"

Her crazed cry would have pierced the heart of a dead man. The boy came back with a frightful flash of agony that was its own anodyne, since it sent him back in the painless dark, to gasp a promise: "With . . . you . . . cheerin' . . . me. . . ."

He thought he was riding Hell-Gait again. And so did she, now that he had brought back the memory. While the wind wailed through the evergreens over them, she rocked him monotonously in her arms, as at the grandstand rail she had rocked herself, her lashes black smudges on her pale face, one white cheek pressed to his, so very white, all the while cheering him: "Jess, I'm with you! I'm with you, Jess!"

So they were when the posse found them.

XV
"THE HIGHROAD"

The melancholy days were gone. November's plains, all brown and sere, its naked groves, and drab, drear desolation, lay under the sparkling white mantle that December had thrown. Big Smoky was so clean that it shone, and the great white peaks so bright in the sun that the eye of mortal could not look upon them. The whole aspect of the range was changed.

Changed, too, was Big Smoky's opinion of Jess Trailor. He was a hero. Alone, wanted himself on a false charge, he had run down the rustlers. He had been instrumental in the capture and death of Spike Travis, their ringleader. And did not that prove that there was some law of recompense? For Spike had made a dying confession that it was his shot that had killed Ute Trailor.

Jess had been shot by the escaping rustler, almost losing his life, in their service. Jetta Fergus had been there, and nearly lost her mind over it. She had got the idea, poor girl, that she had shot him and had suffered a breakdown in consequence, and been confined to her room ever since. Yes, it was quite a romance. It seemed she and Jess had been fond of each other from childhood. Well, she could go a lot further and fare worse. Fine lad — Jess. Good blood — if he was a Trailor. Must have had a superior mother. Still, old Ute might not have been so bad himself. Just got sidetracked somewhere along life's line. A good man gone wrong.

As though to make up for the way it had treated Jess, Big Smoky could not now do enough for him. Not only was his escapade in breaking their jail forgotten, but the people were considering some suitable way to reward him. Folks who had once all but torn the living heart from his breast, who had not been able to see him when he stood right before them, now kept the trail hot to his cabin, bearing gifts and clamoring to see him. Ford, who was caring for him, complained that his legs were " 'most run off" answering the door, and that he would have to build an annex if they didn't quit "cartin' up knick-knacks."

"They won't be satisfied, now," he grumbled to Jess, "till they kill you with kindness."

For old Ford was jealous. He was jealous of all these new friends, who might win the boy from him, of Jack Thorne, who rode up to see Jess every day, and was in there with him now; of the doctor, who had camped there for weeks while the boy's life was despaired of. He had been shot in the same place, Ford would grumble to Jess, and he hadn't been half as sick, and it was lucky they got rid of the doctor when they did. But all the while he fussed over the boy, as solicitously as a cat with one kitten, and a sick one at that.

But Jess had not said anything in reply. He just lay on his cot and looked out at the hills, with a "don't-give-a-hoot" look in his eyes that scared Ford worse than a dozen bullet holes. What had happened up there that night? Had Met got him, or had the girl he loved really shot him? Ford had not asked.

But in the other room, at that moment, Jack Thorne was asking. "Who shot at you, Jess?"

The boy turned his haunted eyes to the window.

"Was it the other rustler?" Thorne pressed, and was filled with remorse at the misery in the boy's pale face when he turned toward him.

"Thorne," Jess pointed to the table, "there's my badge. Take it. There's things about that night I can't ever tell you."

Thorne studied him keenly. But putting two and two together, he had pieced out the truth pretty well for himself, and, seeing Jess's attitude now, he decided that, for all concerned, the ends of justice might better be served by dropping the case.

"As to that," he said slowly, "use your own judgment. I'll trust it. I've lived long enough, boy, to know that some things are better not told. But I don't want your resignation. I've got other work, Jess. And I'm authorized by the association to appoint a permanent deputy here. I want you for the job."

Quickly, almost as desperately as he had refused the first job this man offered, Jess refused it. He could not take it.

"Why not?" Thorne was surprised, for he had thought it an ideal arrangement.

"I . . . I'm goin' away myself," the boy faltered. "Don't tell Ford. He'd want to go . . . an' I can't take him."

"Where are you goin'?" Thorne showed genuine interest.

"I don't know," was the low response. "Anywhere . . . so it's far."

After a moment, his fingers nervously plucking at the Navajo blanket over him, Jess said thoughtfully: "Thorne, ain't it funny how things turn out? I used to care a heap about what home folks thought of me. Now they know I ain't poison . . . I ain't carin'."

No, it was not funny to Thorne. "I'm sorry, boy." That was all he could say. "Sorry for you . . . an', yes, a little bit sorry for myself, too. I really do need a good man here."

"I know a good man." For the first time since his injury Jess showed animation. "The very man for you, Thorne. He helped me with this work. An' if you hunted over sixteen states, you couldn't find a better one."

The range official smiled at this enthusiasm. "Who is your paragon?"

"Ford Cruze!"

Thorne's face lighted, too. "That is an idea!" he exclaimed, for he had come to know Ford very well, and, like all who knew him, had developed a fondness for him.

Without any formalities, he called Ford in and told him that he had been appointed Big Smoky's special deputy for the Cattle Association.

From force of habit Ford flared up: "Not on a bet!"

"But you've already been one," Jess pointed out eagerly. "Or, just the same as one. An' it wasn't so bad. Think it over, Ford."

Now that he had a moment to get used to the idea, Ford more than liked it. He liked living honestly. If he was to go on with Jess, as he was determined to, he had to have a job, and this one. . . .

"But I couldn't take it," he said, turning on Thorne, an old face full of misery, "without tellin' you what I've been. Then you wouldn't let me."

Thorne laid a kindly hand on his arm. "Ford, some of the best men in the West came here because we don't ask what they've been . . . only what they are." Relying again on the instinct that had never failed him, he pinned the badge of office on Ford Cruze. But not inside his coat.

"Where it will show." The old fellow was childish about it. "You know," he mused, as he fingered it proudly, "when I was a kid, I used to dream about bein' a policeman."

So that was settled, and old Ford's feet were out of the mud, and he was on solid ground where he could stand with Jess, not knowing that Jess was going away. The boy was glad, for it eased his mind about Ford — made it easier to leave him.

Late that same day, as Jess lay counting the red mountain-ash berries nodding in at the pane, counting the days when he would be able to go away, Ford came in.

"Feel up to seein' a visitor, son?" he asked queerly.

"Sure."

Yet Ford lingered, eying him, as if he was not sure.

"Son, it's Jim Fergus. I'd 'a' showed him the down trail . . . only I . . . I hadn't the heart."

Jess understood the reason when the Seven Star rancher was ushered in.

He had been expecting Fergus ever since folks had been let in to see him, and had wondered why he had not come. Now that Fergus stood before him, Jess hardly knew him. He was old — old as the hills. His hair was as white as the snow that lay on the hills. And his face — oh, there were plenty of lines of mercy in it. Also, a certain dignity that was pathetic, considering that he had come to beg of a Trailor.

He did not offer to shake hands, but at Jess's request took the chair beside the cot. And there was real concern in his query: "How are you, Jess?"

"Fit to be tied," the boy said, unsmiling.

"That's fine." Fergus sounded as if he meant it. Well, he naturally would on Jetta's account.

A queer, miserable silence fell. Slowly the rancher swung his hat between his knees, scanning the boy, who as frankly returned his gaze. Jess did not hate Fergus any more — had not done so since he had learned that it was Spike who killed his father. He was Jetta's father, and, if there was going to be any more hate, Fergus would have to do it. He was tired of hating. Besides, he would not be here to. . . .

"Jess," Fergus asked suddenly, and all his long and terrible strain was plain, "have you told anyone who was with Spike that night?"

210

The boy shook his head.

The man was pitiable in his relief. "Why didn't you, Jess?" When he got no reply, he began to speak fast, like a man who did not know just what he was saying. "Jess, I know it was Met. I knew it that night. I . . . I reckon I'd have killed you to keep others from knowin' it. Met's left . . . he kept right on goin'. Jetta's had a letter from him. He's in Canada. I wish I could show you that letter, Jess. He owned up to everything . . . what he done to you. Boy, I didn't have a hand in that. What he done to me. . . . He didn't ask my pardon . . . said he wasn't fit yet. Says he may never come home, but if he does, he'll come a man." The rancher's voice broke; his shoulders shook. All his love for his erring son was in his anguished cry of faith: "He'll come!"

Long it rang in the room, filling another miserable interlude.

"Jess, I'm to blame," Fergus broke out again. "What Met is, I made him. I give him his head, an' he done what any headstrong colt would have done . . . run over me, all of us. Oh, I see it. Jetta opened my eyes. She said, if I'd paid more heed to Met an' less to you, this wouldn't have happened. She was right. I was always afraid Met would take up with you, an' you'd influence him bad. Plain talk, Jess . . . but that's what I come for. I just had appearances to go on, an' they was dead against you. I judged you by Ute an' Dan. An' I went berserk when Dan killed my nephew. Sid was like. . . ."

Fiercely the boy checked him. "I'm tryin' not to judge you by Met! An' Dan was good . . . more good than bad. So was Dad! They got off wrong. Dan didn't plan to kill Sid . . . he done it to save his own life."

"I know." Fergus lifted his wintry face. "I don't hold it

against him now. Who am I to hold anything against
anyone? I'm sorry . . . that's what I'm tryin' to tell you. Jess,
my girl told me about that night. You ain't holdin' it against
her?"

The boy's choked cry — "Heaven knows I ain't!" — confirmed all that Jim Fergus had guessed.

"Waal" — he squared his shoulders, as though to prepare them for a heavier weight — "what's done is done.
We've got to look ahead. On Jetta's account, Jess, I'm goin'
to ask you not to tell anyone about Met. . . . No, I showed
you no mercy. Now, I got no right to ask such a favor from
you."

"You needn't." This from the boy he had wronged. "I
don't ever mean to tell on Met."

Jim Fergus drew his first free breath in weeks. He
thanked Jess briefly, and they talked on. It was the first time
he had ever really talked to Jess, and he felt strongly that attraction the boy possessed for all who knew him, understood how a woman could love him. Yes, and a man. . . .

Impulsively, surprising himself, he drew his chair closer,
and laid a rough palm on Jess's hand. "Boy," he said, "I
want to make up to you what I can. Not bribe you, savvy?
Or even try to pay you for what you done, but just an
honest man's wish to pay his debt as far as he can. I'll
winner at that, Jess . . . for you're just the man I want. You
see, boy, I need a foreman out at the Seven Star . . . wait."
The boy had jerked his hand free. "If you believe I'm sin-
cere . . . as sorry as a man can be . . . if you're big enough to
forgive me, then. . . ."

"It ain't that," Jess said.

"Then . . . what is it?" wondered Fergus.

Jess looked him straight in the eye. "I'll talk plain, too. I
. . . I'm plumb loco over Jetta. Always was, an' always will

be. I can't help it, an' I don't want to. An' I couldn't go to the Seven Star, where I'd be seein' her every day. I couldn't stand it."

The rancher grinned — actually. "That's queer talk from a lovesick waddy."

"I can't stand it to stay on the same range, even," said Jess, looking out at the gleaming white hills. "So I'm goin' away."

"Waal," Fergus said dryly, "I ain't inflictin' my daughter on anybody who can't stand her company. I'm mighty loco about her myself . . . now that I've found her."

"You tell her good bye for me," begged Jess, not looking back. "Tell her I wouldn't have taken Met . . . that I'd just found out I couldn't, an' was trying to tell her, when she. . . . Tell her I found I loved her more than I hated you-all. Tell her I said good bye, an'. . . ."

"Whoa!" Fergus got out of his chair. "You're overloadin' my memory. Anyhow, she won't relish a second-hand good bye from you. I'll call her in, an' you tell her."

He went to the door, pausing there to remark casually: "If, by any chance, you should change your mind, come out to the ranch. I sure do need a good foreman."

He left, and a fit of trembling seized Jess. *Call her in. Then she must be here . . . out there with Ford. . . .*

No, she was in the door, coming to him, white as a snowflake herself, and with a look in her eyes to break a man's heart. She walked right past the chair and dropped down by the cot, hid her face in his breast, sobbing out like a child: "I . . . I didn't mean to do it, Jess. It just went off by itself."

Suddenly Jess knew he wasn't going anywhere but to the Seven Star. His arms flashed lovingly around her.

"Hold up your head," tremblingly he bade her.

She did. Her face was as rosy as the red berries against the window. Her eyes were so bright that they shamed the sparklingest peak, and in them shone a light that put the boy of the little blue cañon — that Jess Trailor who Big Smoky had once despised, but now idolized — on a road so high that it led right into heaven.

Cherry Wilson enjoyed a successful career as a Western writer for twenty years. She produced over two hundred short stories and short novels, numerous serials, five hardcover books, and six feature films were based on her fiction. Readers of *Western Story Magazine*, the highest paying of the Street & Smith publications where Wilson was a regular contributor, held her short stories in high regard. Wilson moved from Pennsylvania with her parents to the Pacific Northwest when she was sixteen. She led a nomadic life for many years and turned to writing fiction when her husband fell ill. The first short story she sent to *Western Story Magazine* was accepted, and this began a long-standing professional relationship. If thematically Wilson's Western fiction is similar to that of B. M. Bower, stylistically her stories are less episodic and, as her experience grew, exhibit a greater maturity of sensibility. Her early work, especially, parallels Bower rather closely in that she developed a series of interconnected tales about a group of ranch-hands. There is also a similar emphasis on male bonding and comedic scenes. Wilson stressed human relationships in preference to gun play and action. In fact, some of her best work can be found in those stories that deal with relationships between youngsters and men, as in her novel, *Stormy* (1929), and short stories such "Ghost Town Gold" which has been collected in *The Morrow Anthology of Great Western Short Stories* (1997). Three of Wilson's novels served as the basis for the Buck Jones production unit at Universal Pictures in the 1930s. *Empty Saddles* (1929) and *Thunder Brakes* (1929), book publications of serials first appearing in *Western Story Magazine*, are among her finest Western novels. Most recently much of her finest Western fiction has been appearing for the first time in book form attracting contemporary readers: *Outcasts of Picture Rocks* (1999), *The Throwback* (2002), and *Starr of the Southwest* (2004), consisting of two short novels featuring the same characters, each of which was released as a motion picture. An extraordinary novel titled *Eagle Strange* will be published as a Five Star Western in 2013.